THE GHOST OF BRANDEN BAY

A GHOST COZY MYSTERY

KELLY MASON

LITTLE ORCHARD PRESS®

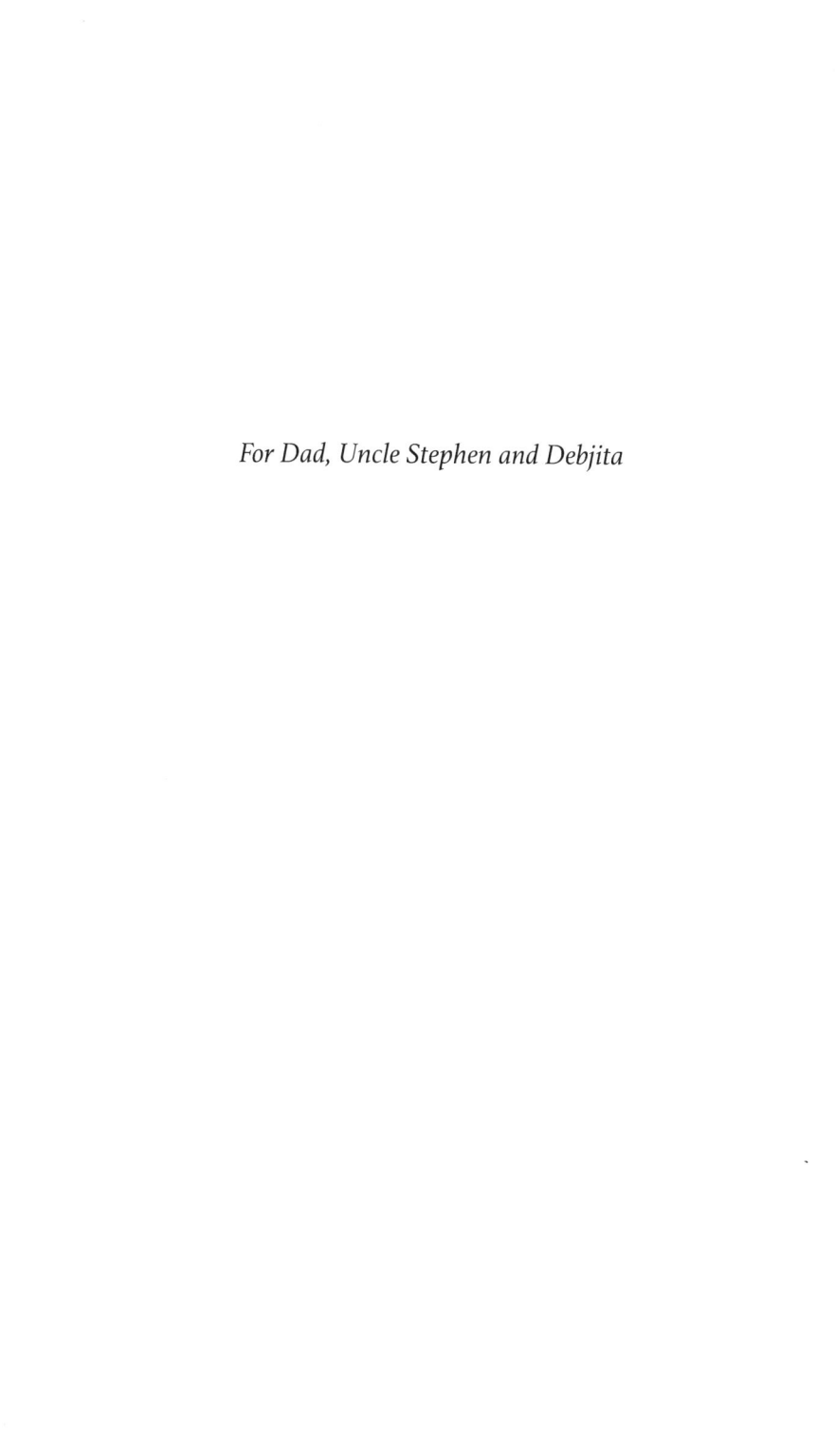

For Dad, Uncle Stephen and Debjita

A NOTE FROM THE AUTHOR

Hi, I hope you enjoy this book. If you would like to know when future books in the series are released, feel free to sign up for my newsletter at:

www.kellymasonbooks.com

"*U*rgh!" Dannie pulled a face. "Look at the sink! I can't share a bathroom with him. When's he leaving?"

"Shh," I said, because Jeff was only in the next room. "*He* has a name. And *Jeff* said he's staying here until he finds somewhere suitable."

Dannie continued. "I feel uncomfortable with him around the place."

Hearing a meow and feeling soft fur against my legs, I bent down, picking up Constance. My cat nuzzled her face against mine.

"You can move into my room and use the en-suite," I said to Dannie, sounding a lot brighter than I felt on the inside. I hated the idea of giving up that bedroom.

Constance gave an angry wail and I grinned at her. She always meowed in all the right places, as if she understood. I didn't blame her for protesting. It had been Grandma's bedroom and was the best in the house. Decorated in an ornate Victorian fashion, it provided views of Branden Bay's promenade from a plush chaise lounge placed in the bay window. I loved fetching a hot drink in the morning and sitting there, watching my world slowly wake up.

"I feel bad." Dannie lowered her chin, then looked up at me sheepishly. "I'll pay more rent?"

"You haven't given me a penny towards it yet." I laughed.

"But you're going to keep back some of my reward money, aren't you? Like I suggested."

I was receiving a reward after recovering a haul of diamonds and planned to share it with everyone who'd helped solve the mystery. To be fair, Dannie also helped me with my bookkeeping and the café, so I'd never asked her for rent.

"Are we swapping rooms? The one I've been sleeping in is a lot smaller."

"No, I'll move in there," I said, pointing to a door which faced the top of the stairs.

Constance jumped to the floor and sashayed towards the closed door and scratched at it.

"The one full of junk?" Dannie asked. "What are you going to sleep on?"

"Believe it or not, underneath the clutter is a bed," I said. "The room is long overdue a clear out. You've given me a reason to do it."

"Are you going to share the bathroom with Jeff?" she asked.

I shook my head. "There's a huge en-suite bathroom in there. The three of us will have a bathroom each." To be honest, as much as I blamed Dannie for being a drama queen, I didn't fancy sharing a bathroom with Jeff, either. I viewed him as the kid brother I'd never had, but was fed up with telling him to pick up his cartoon-covered clothes from the floor. In fact, since Dannie and Jeff moved in with me, I was feeling more like their mother than their landlady and I was only six years older than them.

"Are you sure?" Dannie asked.

"Of course." *Bang goes my relaxing day off*, I thought. I had a hair appointment and massage booked at Millar's, Branden Bay's poshest hotel and spa. I'd have to cancel them both. Sighing, I smoothed my red locks, which were getting rather long. I never seemed to have the time to get them cut. I gave a breezy smile, not wanting Dannie to feel guilty.

"Thanks, Becky," she said, then turned as Jeff's door opened.

He appeared on the landing, pale from being forever indoors having spent most of his youth watching on-line videos on ghost hunting. Dannie frowned as her gaze rested on his superman emblazoned underpants and I made a mental note to buy him a dressing gown for his upcoming birthday.

Jeff rubbed his bare belly as if dreaming of breakfast. "You two up to anything interesting today?"

Fearful that Dannie would snap something sarcastic at him, I jumped in. "I'm clearing out the spare room. Would you like to help?"

"Sure," he said, and scratched the stubble on his chin, which matched the sandy hair on his head.

Dannie flicked her long blonde hair over her shoulders and walked away.

"Can I use your van?" I asked, knowing the answer would be yes, as Jeff would do anything for me. Lynn, my psychic neighbour, had told me that for every medium like myself, there is a gatekeeper, someone to protect them. Jeff overheard this and decided that his life's purpose was to be my right-hand man and protector. I was pretty sure he wasn't *the one*, but it seemed to make him happy.

"Of course, boss," he said.

I swallowed as I looked at the closed door, but a part of me was looking forward to moving in there, because it had been my room when I'd visited as a child.

HALF AN HOUR LATER, Jeff and I surveyed the furniture and boxes of bric-à-brac as Constance rubbed up against an old chest of drawers.

Jeff gave a low whistle. "There's a lot of stuff in here."

I turned around to face him. "The wardrobe, chest of drawers, bed, dressing table, rocking horse, chair and toy chest are staying, but everything else has to go."

"What, these antiques?" he gestured around the room.

I nodded. "They give me the creeps." I'd collected them up from around the house.

Constance meowed at my feet, looking up with a sorrowful expression.

Bending down, I stroked her. "I've already discussed it with my dad, and we agreed. It's silly keeping them locked away when there are plenty of people out there who would appreciate them."

"You might make a tidy sum," Jeff said, as he held a large white and blue ceramic vase.

I nodded and lifted Constance, scratching her head. "I'll call the auction house."

JEFF PULLED the van away as it creaked with its heavy load. We had taken the larger pieces of furniture, having moved the bric-a-brac into the attic for another day. Constance sat in my tote bag by my feet. She had a habit of following me everywhere and people around town were becoming used to seeing us together, with her head poking out of one of the many designer tote bags I'd inherited from Grandma. Jeff was about to turn into the High Street, but we found a crowd blocking the entrance, many were carrying placards.

"What's that all about?" I asked.

"The betting shop that's supposed to be opening," Jeff replied. "Two guys from work are here, supporting their mother." Jeff had a part-time job at a large D.I.Y store. He opened the window and stuck his head out.

"Ollie. Doug," he called, then waved at a couple of guys.

A woman shouted out. "No to gambling!"

"Not on our High Street," the crowd joined in.

"Ah yes, of course," I said, remembering an article I'd read about the proposed betting shop in the Gazette. "Why's it turning into a near riot?"

"The Council vote on it this Thursday."

"I can't see them allowing it," I said.

Jeff continued along the seafront, taking the long way around town, being careful with his driving so not to damage our load. Rain pattered against the windscreen, and it didn't bode well for my café business. The forecast was poor for the entire week and with no clear skies above, the sea looked grey rather than the blue of recent weeks.

After a slow drive, we reached the auction house. It was on the outskirts of Hedgebury Village, halfway from home to Bristol. It was a single-storey building, converted from stables. We stopped in the gravel car park.

"I'll get the auctioneer," I said. "I've arranged for him to look at the items in the van as there's no point in us dragging it all in if he can't sell it. You stay here," I said. "And keep a hold of Constance."

Jeff reached for my cat. "Okay, boss."

As I entered, I spotted the auctioneer through the window of his office door. I recognised him immediately from his website. His name was Adrian Shaw, and he wore a suit, which looked circa 1940s with a cravat.

Adrian was in his thirties and had a shock of dark hair. He completed his look with gold-rimmed glasses. I remained outside the door for a while as he chatted away to a customer, a tall, grey-haired man who had his back to me. They seemed to be deep in conversation so I decided to go for a wander. I went into the auction room full of sofas, cabinets, and long tables, upon which were all manner of items which caught my eye. As I wound up an ornately carved music box, I heard the customer shouting.

"Five hundred? I've had it valued at five thousand!"

I placed the box down as it played a tinkling Edelweiss.

"Just do your best," the person shouted.

Jeff approached with Constance in his arms. "You okay, boss? You've been a while."

"As you can hear, Adrian is busy with someone."

"The cat was going crazy."

Constance wriggled in his clutches and growled.

"Here," I said stretching out my arms. "Calm down, Connie." I squeezed her close, then turned around as I heard the customer stomping away.

Adrian approached, grinning at me. "Ah, Becky James, the psychic detective." He waved his arms around, as if he'd just magicked me up as part of a conjuring show. "Apologies, I was longer with the previous customer than I expected."

"He didn't sound too happy," Jeff said.

"He brought in this brooch." Adrian opened his hands to reveal an array of blue stones in a gold setting. "It's a delightful piece. Beautifully preserved. But some people think insurance valuations point to the true value of an item." He shook his head. "Those valuations never meet expectations at auction." He popped the brooch into his breast pocket, then rubbed his hands together. "I'm so chuffed you came in. I like to dabble with the occult myself. Maybe we could team up for a séance?" He gestured around the room, nearly knocking Jeff's head. "A lot of the furniture that passes through here has attachments."

I shuddered. I wanted to keep him on side and needed to get the best price possible for the items I'd brought along, but I was having no part in anything which involved calling up the dead. "Jeff here is running a few ghost hunts, aren't you?"

"Yes. I'm getting booked up," Jeff said. "But I'm setting up new events all the time." He looked around the room. "Or we could do something here?" He stared at the array of antiques, rubbing his chin. "If you have anything possessed."

Constance jumped to the ground and hissed at the door of an old wardrobe.

The auctioneer took a step backwards. "The psychic cat. I read about her in the Gazette." He turned to the wardrobe, put his hands to his mouth, mimicking a megaphone, and spoke in a spooky voice. "Is there anyone there?"

Oh, no. I shook my head. The last thing I wanted was this trip to turn into some sort of paranormal investigation. I'd accepted that my life was going to be interrupted by spirits seeking the truth, but I had no intention of looking for them.

I nodded at Jeff. "I'm sure Jeff has one of his business cards on him?"

Jeff pulled a card from his pocket but dropped it on the floor.

I leaned down and picked it up. On the front was *Becky James Paranormal Detective Agency*, and underneath that, *Jeff Smith, Chief Investigator,* followed by his mobile number. I raised my eyebrows and put a hand on my hip. What on earth was he doing using my name for his business?

"I got them printed last week. Great, aren't they?" His cheeks were tinged with pink.

I glared at him until the pink deepened to burgundy. "Not really," I said. "But we'll discuss it later."

"I thought you liked purple," Jeff mumbled.

True, it had a nice juxtaposing effect on my red hair and green eyes, but I gave him one of those 'just wait until I get you home' stares my mother was fond of, then turned to Adrian as he pocketed the card. "Maybe you could value the items I've brought? They're in the van."

ON OUR WAY back to Branden Bay, I gave Jeff a bit of a roasting for using my name for his paranormal investigation business. He used the excuse that his bookings had gone through the roof, and he'd give me a cut. I suggested he saved it for a deposit on a place of his own and he went rather quiet.

Back home, in my kitchen, I felt guilty for being so harsh, so offered him a slice of cake. "Try my latest addition to the menu. It's a passionfruit and pistachio cake."

He accepted the generous serving I handed him.

I took a bite myself. The sponge was moist with a passionfruit drizzle, sandwiched with a pistachio butter cream. It was divine and Jeff loved it, wolfing it down. As I watched him, a warmth came over me, reminding me to lighten up. The fact was, even though I often craved privacy, it was nice having Dannie and Jeff around the place. It livened the house up and gave it a less spooky feel.

I poured the tea as we sat at the table. "So, what are you doing for your birthday?"

He sighed. "Mum wants to take me out for a meal and bingo."

"What for your twenty-first? That doesn't sound like much fun. I'll do a small get-together for you here with the gang."

"Are you sure? Mum can't take me on my actual birthday, anyway. We're going out on Thursday. That's her Bingo night."

"Of course. I'll invite everyone over for Friday, then." We finished our cake and tea before venturing up to my new room.

As I opened the door of the bedroom, I took a sharp intake of breath.

Dannie had made up the bed and was dusting. "I thought I'd start it for you," she said.

Memories of my childhood came flashing back. Lying in the small double bed, with Grandma sat beside me on the soft green velvet armchair, reading me a bedtime story. I felt a tear in my eye as Constance jumped onto the chair and meowed.

"Are you okay?" Dannie asked. "I haven't upset you, have I?"

I cleared my throat. "I'm fine. Just reminiscing."

Jeff scanned the room. "It's massive in here."

"It doubled up as my playroom." I glanced at the rocking horse in front of the fireplace, then walked across the room to a baby pink coloured door with peeling paint and pushed it open. Inside was a huge, white cast-iron bath, over which was a large shower-head at the end of a long, curved pipe. I pulled back the rather mouldy-looking shower curtain and leaned over, turning on the taps. The water came out in fits and spurts until it ran in a continuous flow. I then flushed the toilet, which had a chain with a wooden handle. It worked fine, although there was a groaning afterward, due to air in the pipes.

"It's all working," Jeff said.

"It needs a deep clean, a new shower curtain and bathmats." I turned around to face him. "That's it, Jeff. I can take it from here with Dannie."

"Are you sure?" he asked.

I nodded and put a hand on his arm. "Thanks for taking me to the auction rooms."

I turned back to the bath, feeling emotional, remembering Grandma washing my hair as she sang me songs. She'd been an actress and singer. No-one could sing as beautifully as Grandma. Taking in a deep breath, I got to work. There was cleaning to do and then an awful lot of baking.

CHAPTER 2

"Hi, Mrs Jessup, what can I get you?" I asked my neighbour as she sat at her favourite table. She came into the café every day to devour a chapter of whatever book she was reading.

"What's your special, love?" Mrs Jessup asked.

"This week I have a passionfruit and pistachio cake and Jeff has given it his seal of approval."

"Yes please, dear. That sounds super."

After asking her about her book, I got her order ready. Mrs Jessup had taken a liking to Earl Grey tea with lemon. As I filled the teapot with hot water from my shiny commercial drinks machine – which I'd spent a small fortune on – Lynn sidled up to me. She was in her fifties with bushy, shoulder-length hair, a mixture of silver and blonde. She ran a spiritualist church which backed onto my garden. She'd helped me out so much with the café at the beginning and was now working for me on a permanent basis.

"You get off on your break, lovey, I'll take Mrs Jessup's order over."

"She's having the passionfruit," I said, knowing how much Mrs Jessup liked a natter with Lynn.

As Lynn cut the cake, I placed the pot of tea on a tray. "I'm texting out invites to Jeff's party in my break."

"I can't wait. It'll be marvellous. We haven't all been together since your last case." She placed a slice of cake on a plate and then cut another. "Have you had any sightings recently?"

I shook my head. "No. Thank goodness," I said as I made myself a cappuccino. "Trust me, that's a good thing. The only spirits I've seen so far have been those of murdered people."

Lynn placed the second slice of cake on a plate. "Of course, lovey." I was sure I could sense a tinge of disappointment in her voice. "Here." She passed me a slice.

I took it with my drink through to the snug, a small lounge at the back of the house with French windows that led out to my garden. Constance lay on the side of the armchair, pawing at large raindrops running down the window. She turned her head and acknowledged me, then swiped at a large droplet, as if she was sulking. A couple of months before, she'd been involved in a knife attack and I'd been over-protective of her ever since. Everyone had been moaning at me to let her out again.

"Cats are wild. They have legal freedom to roam the land," Dannie had said. I wasn't convinced that Dannie had any interest in feline rights and suspected it was because she no longer wanted to empty the litter tray. But she had a point, and the person who stabbed Constance was in prison awaiting trial, and my cat's belly was completely healed.

I sat on the sofa. Lynn had added a fork to my plate with the cake and I needed it for the beautiful passion-fruit drizzle. I shut my eyes as my mouth filled with sweetness. *Yum.* Once I'd finished my cake and coffee, I texted invitations to the gang for Jeff's birthday party. First there was Izzy. She was an ex-model and the local newspaper reporter. Then Annie, a manager at the pier. They were both away on a brief trip to London.

I texted Dannie, as she hadn't surfaced from her new bedroom all day. There was a desk in there and I assumed she was using it to study at, having enrolled on a bookkeeping course.

I hesitated, the last member of the gang was Detective Sergeant Henry Blake, known to his friends as H. I sighed, recalling that for the past four months everyone had been suggesting that we had some sort of magnetic attraction. I'd pushed that aside as rubbish, not realising until it was too late that I'd been blind-sided by an unpleasant break-up from my boss/boyfriend Marcus back in London. H had hooked up with a glamorous gym instructor called Tara before I could tell him exactly how I felt. I was stuck firmly in his friend zone and felt miserable about it.

Tara, who was typically tall to my short, with sleek chestnut hair, had made me more than a tad jealous. Truth was, they looked the perfect match. But I had to put my feelings aside. It was Jeff's birthday not a party for me, and I needed to invite them both. I texted an invite to H, hesitating before adding, *Tara's welcome.*

The sun broke out of the clouds, and I stood up, opening the French windows.

"Go on then." I smiled as I watched Constance step onto the paving outside and sniff the air.

My phone dinged. H had texted right back.

Great to hear from you. Can I pop over at about three? I'd like us to have a chat xx

The two kisses did not go unnoticed by me. Maybe things were not going well with Tara after all? *Slow down,* I told myself. I intended to carry on as cool as I'd always been. Still, I felt a tickling sensation inside.

JUST BEFORE THREE, Lynn approached me as I took a contactless payment. We'd been busier since the sun had come out from the clouds and dried up the paths.

"I'll take over. You get out the back and I'll send H through when he arrives." Her eyes danced. Seeing as she was psychic, there was no hiding my feelings from her, even though I continued to deny them outwardly.

"I'll be in the garden, send him through when he arrives," I said, removing my apron, then smoothing my hair. I didn't want to look like I'd done myself up, so just added a swipe of lipstick and left it at that.

From the kitchen, I spied Constance lying on the bench, situated under the apple tree, which was now showing small fruit. I was looking forward to them being ripe enough to pick. I opened the back door and walked up the lawn and settled on the bench, stroking my cat, and wondering what apple recipes I could introduce to the café. Anything to stop my mind guessing what H wanted to talk to me about. After all, it might be something totally bland, like preparing a buffet for a police meeting.

After two minutes, Lynn appeared at the back door. *He's early?* I thought.

"There's someone to see you, lovey." She gestured behind her. "He says he's your boyfriend?"

I raised my eyebrows. H must have ended it with Tara. But it was very presumptuous of him to assume that I would say yes to being his girlfriend without even asking me. Still, his forwardness amused me and I laughed. "Send him out." I stood up and smoothed my top. Then sat down again. *Look casual,* I told myself as I gazed across the expanse of lush grass as if deep in thought.

"Becks."

I froze at the sound of the voice. My heart near stopped in its tracks. Had I imagined it? I looked gingerly towards the back door. No, I hadn't. "What are you doing here?" I said, feeling my temper rising.

Walking towards me was Marcus, my ex from London. "That's no way to greet your boyfriend after not seeing him for four months." He opened his arms as if I'd rush over and embrace him.

I stood up and put my hands on my hips. "You seem to have forgotten. We split up."

"Lots of couples have a trial separation." He approached me with his arms still outstretched.

I raised my arm with the palm of my hand in stop-mode. "That's not what it was, and you know it."

By this time Constance was off the bench and in front of me with her back arched and her long fur so bushed out she looked like a giant hedgehog.

"Look, I gave you some space, and it's worked." He pointed towards the house. "You've done amazing for yourself, setting up a business. And your marketing skills are spot on." He pulled a rolled up national newspaper from his back pocket. "I can't believe you made the Daily News. This paranormal stunt is ace. You're a marketing genius."

My friend Izzy had sold the story of my last case to a national tabloid, as it involved a well-known jewel thief. I groaned. "The story was exaggerated."

"Obviously. I know you, Becks, we were together for three years. You're not psychic. But it's amazing. You're a household name around here," he said. "I'm not sure why I didn't notice your marketing skills over the years."

I gritted my teeth. "Clearly, seeing as you gave the job you promised me, to someone else."

"That's all water under the bridge, babe. I want you to come back to the firm as a senior marketing executive."

"No thanks." I crossed my arms. "I'm done with London and as you've seen, I've my own business."

"What, this little café?" He looked behind him and

then back at me. "You can sell it as a going concern. The takings must be peanuts out in the backwater, compared to what you'd make in the city. You'll be on six figures in no time if you bring a bunch of new clients to the firm."

"I thought that was your job?"

"Okay, you'd be assisting me. But come on." He held out his hands. "We'd be the dream team."

Constance growled, moved forward, and hissed at Marcus.

"Whose cat is that?"

"Mine. And the answer is no."

"Don't scowl, Becks. I don't want to be paying out for Botox to iron your wrinkles out."

I thrust my arms by my sides, my hands clenched into fists.

"Wow. You've bloomed." He cocked his head to one side, staring at my torso. "Really filled out."

Okay, so I'd put on a few pounds. For goodness' sake, I was a baker. I had to try out the goods. I crossed my arms over my chest. "It's time for you to go."

Lynn appeared at the door. "Are you okay, lovey?"

"Marcus was just leaving," I called out.

Constance gave a low wail as her tail swished from side to side, then launched herself at Marcus's leg.

"Ouch, get this thing off me," he cried out like a baby, with his arms up in the air, shaking the shin that Constance clutched onto. He wore jeans, so she didn't sink her teeth into any flesh – more's the pity.

I leaned forward to retrieve her, knowing that

Marcus was the type to report my cat as a dangerous animal and demand a lethal injection. "Come on, Constance, I can handle this creep."

Lynn came towards me. "I'll take her."

"Where'd you get that cat from?" Marcus asked. "The zoo?"

"Don't insult my pet. She shows a lot more loyalty than you ever did."

"Becks," Marcus said to me.

"Don't call me that. I hate it." I passed a hissing Constance to Lynn.

"Babe, come on, chill." His voice softened. "Let's have a heart to heart." He gave a small smile. "I didn't realise I'd hurt you so bad."

"H is here," Lynn said as she attempted to calm my cat.

My shoulders drooped. I turned to Marcus. "Leave. Go out the back." I pointed to the rear stone wall where a gate was.

I looked back to the house when H appeared, nearly filling the whole doorway. He smiled at me, then frowned as his gaze rested upon Marcus, then back to me.

I felt my cheeks burn bright red.

"Are you okay?" H called out.

I opened my mouth, but I couldn't find anything to say as Marcus strode over to him.

"I'd better get back to the café, lovey," Lynn said, as she struggled with Constance, who swiped her paws in Marcus's direction. H stepped onto the patio to let

Lynn pass, as Marcus reached him. I stared at them standing together. They were the same height but opposites. H, dark hair, broad chest, wearing a tight black T-shirt and black jeans. His hair shining naturally. Marcus, blonde, gelled hair, willowy and in a long-sleeved blue shirt, tucked into blue denim jeans with a tan belt which matched his shoes. *Why did I never notice?* I thought. *He dresses just like my dad.*

"And you are?" H growled at Marcus, clearly sensing my discomfort.

"I'm Becks's boyfriend. We've been together for three years." Marcus turned back to me and grinned. "Haven't we, babe?"

H's chest appeared to grow, like a bear's about to attack.

I swallowed and opened my mouth.

Before I could speak, Marcus continued. "Hasn't she mentioned me?"

"I … er …" My mouth felt dry and my words ran out.

"No," H said. "She hasn't"

"And you are?" Marcus asked.

"Detective Sergeant Blake," H said through gritted teeth.

Marcus stepped back. "She's not in any trouble is she, officer?"

"Am I interrupting something?" H said to me in a gruff voice.

I didn't know what to say as he glowered in my direction. I hadn't mentioned Marcus to any of my new friends at all. Not even to Lynn. I'd attempted to erase him from my memory because I didn't like the bitter feeling I had every time I thought of him. And now, it looked as if I'd been hiding a secret. I needed to have it out with Marcus, but not with anyone watching.

"I'll call you later," I said to H.

"Are you sure you're okay?" he asked.

I nodded. "I'll text you."

Marcus turned around as soon as H went. "You're not romancing that meat suit, are you?"

I breathed out and counted to ten in my head. "Just leave, and never come here again."

"Hey, calm down. I'm sorry, babe." He approached me. "I know it's a bit of a shock. Look. Meet me tonight for dinner. Hear me out. If you don't want the job, after I've told you all about it, I'll go away and you'll never see me again."

As much as I hated the idea of dining with Marcus, the last thing I wanted was him endlessly pestering me. I knew what he was like. He would have kept on and on until I'd listened to his pitch.

"Where?" I crossed my arms again.

"The Italian on the High Street. At seven thirty?"

"If you promise that after I've heard what you've got to say, you'll leave town?"

"I promise."

I showed Marcus out the back way, through the gate, and told him how to get back to Millar's, where he told me he was staying. I watched as he left. I planned to listen to his job offer, take advantage of the meal, and get a few things off my chest at the same time. As unpleasant as it was, I realised it would be cathartic. A chance for me to have closure.

I pulled my mobile out of my pocket, longing to speak to my friend Annie. She always calmed me down when life threw me a curve ball. But I didn't want to interrupt the fun she and Izzy were no doubt having on their trip. They'd begged me to go too, but having spent three long years at endless client socials with Marcus in London, it didn't have the same appeal. I sighed and texted H, asking him to contact me to rearrange a meet-up for our chat, and told him I'd explain about Marcus. I planned to get the meal with my ex out of the way and then focus on the rest of my life.

CHAPTER 3

*A*s I walked along the seafront, I pulled my purple pashmina around my shoulders. The clouds were dark and there was no orange sunset that evening. I realised I should have worn a coat. As the wind blew, I held onto the skirt of my dress. I knew Marcus liked sleek, crisp shift dresses. At first, when he'd filled my wardrobe with new clothes, I'd been flattered. After a time, I'd realised it was because he wanted to dictate what I wore. This time, I was wearing one of Grandma's floral dresses. It was bright and very country-looking, and the opposite of what Marcus would want to see me in. I'd teamed it with some brightly-coloured sandals. Marcus hated anything which showed toes. He hated feet. I'd painted my toenails purple. He detested purple. I grinned. Okay so maybe I was being childish, but it lightened my mood and would send a simple message to Marcus: *I don't care what you think any more.*

I opened the door to Corelli's wine bar and bistro. A waft of garlic hit me and my tummy rumbled. This was my favourite place to eat out. *Let's get this done,* I told myself, then groaned. My bravado seeped away. On a table for two, in the centre of the restaurant, were H and Tara. Yep, it was a small town, and this was the only decent restaurant unless you wanted to pay top dollar up at Millar's hotel. H clocked me and I looked away as the owner, Elena Corelli, approached. She was a beautiful woman with thick, lustrous, dark hair which wouldn't look out of place in a shampoo advert.

"Becky, so nice to see you. Table for one?" she asked in her Italian accent.

"Becks, there you are," Marcus called out.

I turned towards his voice to see him at a table situated at the far wall with a man and woman. I flushed hot. For a moment, I thought he'd brought his equally controlling parents. I squinted and realised, with relief, they were not.

"I'm actually joining that table." My stomach lurched as I nodded towards Marcus. I very much wanted to turn around and go home.

"Okay, I will let you settle, then take your orders."

Feeling hot, I removed my pashmina and placed it on the coat stand, where there were a few raincoats and a tweed flat cap.

Elena led me across the room. The only other customers were a middle-aged couple sitting together at a window table. They looked vaguely familiar, but then so did most people in town, considering how many I saw in the café.

Tara smiled sweetly at me as I passed their table. She looked different. She usually wore her hair up in a ponytail, but on this occasion, it cascaded over her bare shoulders with a few wisps framing her face. I also noticed that she was wearing a tight-fitting white dress. *White?* I thought. *Who wears white to an Italian with all that tomato-filled meat sauce?* I saw a vision in my head of me splattering her with Bolognese, then mentally slapped myself. The jealousy was getting out of hand.

Tara looked me up and down and frowned at my dress.

Okay, I thought. *So maybe it won't only be Marcus that will think I've no sense of fashion.* I gulped. "Hi there," I said to Tara and H.

H stared at me but said nothing.

I dragged my eyes away, with shoulders drooping as I looked ahead at Marcus. *What's he up to?*

Marcus rose from his seat. "Eddie, this is Becky James you've heard so much about." He smiled at the man opposite him as I approached.

I felt as if everyone in the room was staring at me.

Eddie also stood up. He was about five foot ten, wearing a pin-striped suit and had mousey brown hair. "Great to meet you." He stuck out his hand and a waft of cigar-tinged breath hit me. He looked like something out of Bugsy Malone.

"Pleased to meet you," I lied, shaking his damp

hand. I smiled over at his companion, who had dark brown shoulder-length hair, and wore a simple, chic burnt-orange dress. Around her neck was a delicate chain with a single solitaire diamond dangling from it.

"This is the missus," Eddie said.

"Fiona." She smiled at me, appearing to be a million times more sophisticated than her husband.

"I've read the newspaper reports about you," Eddie said.

I groaned inwardly but managed to force a polite smile.

"As you're aware, Eddie is a successful business-man," Marcus chipped in.

What's his game? I thought as I turned and narrowed my eyes at him. I had no idea who this Eddie was. Marcus had clearly dragged me along to a client meeting. Just like the old days. He was unbelievable.

Marcus's Adam's apple bobbed up and down before he continued. "Eddie is considering bringing his accounts to the firm. I've told him you'll be joining us as a senior marketing executive."

My mouth dropped open. "Marcus." Was he using me to bait a client, yet again?

Marcus widened his eyes at me and pointed to the free chair against the wall. "Sit down and have a glass of Prosecco." He sat back down again.

"I know the feeling, Becky," Fiona said, My distaste was clearly on show. "There should be a ban on busi-ness talk after seven p.m."

I looked across to H who glowered at me as he

watched my every move. I shut my eyes. *Great.* I took a deep breath and reopened them as I exhaled slowly.

Marcus poured me a glass of bubbly from a bottle he pulled from an ice bucket. "When in Rome, eh?" he said.

More like Italian Prosecco is cheaper than French Champagne, I thought. Although he rarely held back when he had his hands on the company credit card. I was just about to tell him where to go but I'd been rehearsing my speech on the way up as if I'd been learning lines for a play. I wanted the opportunity to deliver it. I moved to the chair and parked myself on it. I decided to enjoy the food and then tell Marcus exactly what I thought of him once we were alone.

I scanned the room. The middle-aged couple at the window appeared to be having an intense discussion. It was quiet, even for a Tuesday. A petite, blonde waitress came to the table with a large bottle of water and four glasses on a tray. I placed her as being late thirties. As soon as she set eyes on Eddie, the tray shook.

Eddie stared at her, then lifted his glass, taking a gulp of bubbly.

I leaned forward. "I'll take this for you." I picked the bottle up before it tipped over. As I did so, a glass slipped off the tray and smashed on the floor.

"I'm so sorry," the waitress stuttered and hurried off.

"Perfect," Fiona sighed. "Curious career choice for someone who has an issue carrying a tray without dropping it." Fiona stared at her husband as if waiting for him to comment.

He shrugged his shoulders. "At least she's got a job."

"Oh, another dig at me, is it? I don't measure up, do I?" She flicked her hair. "I don't have a job, husband dear, because I have a calling. It's different."

"You say that, like you're the blinking vicar." Eddie turned to me. "Fiona's life revolves around horses. I met her at Bath racecourse."

"Dressage," Fiona said, giving a sweet smile. "Not horse-racing." She looked at Eddie, then back at me. "Father is a racehorse trainer." She took a sip of her drink. "Do you ride, Becky?"

"I've ridden a donkey on Branden Bay beach," I said with a short laugh, which no-one joined in with.

We were interrupted by the sound of the waitress, who was on her hands and knees, sweeping up shattered glass.

Eddie moved forward as if he was going to help, then glanced at Fiona and appeared to think better of it. He took a sip of his drink and sat back in his seat.

The waitress stood up, with blonde ringlets over her flushed face. "I'll be right over to take your food order."

"Can we have a few more minutes?" Marcus asked.

"Oh, okay. Yes. Sure." She hurried away.

Marcus passed me a menu.

I didn't take it; I knew it off by heart. I'd eaten there so many times before. "The lasagne here is amazing.

I'll be having that." I gave a cursory glance at the specials board. There were a couple of dishes I fancied but stuck with my first choice.

"So, when are you moving back to London?" Eddie asked me.

I glanced at Marcus through slitted eyes. There was no way I was going to be playing an acting role in his little game. Instead, I left an awkward silence.

Marcus cleared his throat. "She's got business to attend to here, so will work remotely to start with. Out in the field."

"The Gazette articles about you have been very interesting," Eddie said. "I don't normally read the local rag, but I've been running an advertising campaign in Branden Bay, ahead of launch." He looked over at the couple eating by the window. "Assuming the Council doesn't make trouble."

Marcus jumped in. "Becky's story made the nationals, too."

"So I hear." Eddie turned and raised his glass at me. "You can do so much these days with a high profile. Celebrity is everything and a major influence on success."

I put my hand up. "I'm not interested in any of that." I'd hated the attention I received following Izzy's articles about my so-called gift for seeing the dead. It made me feel like a Victorian circus exhibit.

Fiona sighed. "Eddie is keen to get to know you. He loves any excuse to name drop."

Eddie ignored his wife. "So tell me, did a ghost lead

you to those diamonds?"

Fiona gave a short laugh and shook her head. "Utter rhubarb."

Eddie smiled at me. "So, how long have you had the gift?"

"Only a few months. The truth is," I said. "I'm a reluctant medium. I seem to attract spirits rather than call them up. And I'm not really into entertainment."

Eddie took a gulp of Prosecco and burped.

Fiona rolled her eyes. "I read that you have a performing arts degree."

"She's an excellent actress," Marcus said. "But she landed herself a proper job in the City and grew out of the pipe dream of a life in the West End." Marcus put a hand on my arm. "Didn't you, Becks?"

I narrowed my eyes. Looking back at the years I'd spent with Marcus objectively, I could see that he'd helped to knock my confidence as far as my acting career was concerned. I gave him a stern stare, then turned and smiled at Fiona. "Unfortunately, I wasn't successful in my initial auditions. But I may pursue acting in the future."

Marcus jumped in. "Doesn't pay the bills, though. It's nice to have a regular income." He turned to me. "Eddie and Fiona are in town as they're opening a betting shop as part of their chain."

Oh no, I thought, remembering the placard-carrying protesters Jeff and I had witnessed the previous day, realising I was having dinner with the town's most hated newcomers.

CHAPTER 4

I stared at Marcus and shook my head as he topped up my glass, avoiding my gaze.

"My betting shop will be a couple of doors up," Eddie said. "I've a meeting with the council tomorrow to drum up support before they vote on it Thursday. We're staying over at that Millar's hotel. Nice isn't it?" He turned to his wife. "You could go to the spa tomorrow. Maybe Becky could join you?"

Fiona flicked her hair. "I've a meeting first thing in the morning." She stared at him. "Remember? I'm going back tonight, so I've already booked a car."

"I'm busy with the café," I said quickly, looking from Fiona to Eddie. They appeared mis-matched, and I wondered what the attraction was as I eyed a roll of banknotes in front of Eddie, held in a gold money clip.

"Eddie's planning to open his fortieth shop on his fortieth birthday," Fiona said. "That's why he's in a rush to push things through. It's his birthday next month."

"I saw a protest yesterday. You've had a bit of opposition," I said.

"That woke lot. Saying my shops are bad for mental health? If you have self-control, gambling can launch a career. I won big at the horses and then invested it into my shops. It's been a good thing for me."

Fiona groaned. "Can we stop the talk about business and gambling?"

Eddie ignored her. "Councillor Nigel Levison over there disapproves of my shop." He pointed to the couple seated at the window table. "But I'm still counting on his vote." He laughed. "He's next in line for mayor."

Fiona ran her hand through her hair. "I feel sorry for Branden Bay. They're a dreadful couple."

"It's him that's the problem," Eddie said. "Nothing wrong with Gina."

Fiona gave a short laugh. "His wife is a total nightmare. I've never met someone so cheap, yet she considers herself above her station."

"Come off it, Fi. Levison would be nothing without her. She's got drive," Eddie said. "The reason she doesn't like you is that you came between us."

"Maybe you should have married her instead."

"Don't be ridiculous." Eddie shook his head. "I'm hoping she's going to talk some sense into her husband, so he'll add his vote to approve the shop."

Councillor Levison and his wife Gina gave their orders to Elena. As I watched, I remembered where I'd seen them before. There was an article about their involvement with a Victorian Town Theme Day, which was being organised by the fair owner, Andrew Farr.

"It's the same story in all the small towns," Eddie said. "They say they want to keep their high streets traditional, but gambling has been around for centuries."

"But they didn't open betting shops until the 1960s," I added, having read that in the Gazette. "So, it's not fitting for a Victorian-style high street."

Eddie leaned back in his seat and laced his fingers together. "The punters want them. They enjoy going into a shop for the thrill of the bet and to meet up with their mates. I'm going to keep opening shops until there's a Fly's Flutters on every high street in the country."

Marcus jumped in. "Eddie built his business up in only ten years. He's a true success story."

"It's up to those playing to do it responsibly," Eddie added.

"It can be addictive, though," I said.

"So can food and drink." Eddie leaned forward. "No-one's having a pop at the landlord of this joint."

"The restaurateur is a woman," I said, nodding at Elena.

"Oh, she owns the place, does she? The do-gooders would never have a go at a woman. Us men get all the grief, especially when we're running businesses which rely on our customers' ability to manage their own urges." He spoke so loudly, everyone in the room must have heard.

Nigel Levison's wife stood up, she wore a brown skirt and beige blouse. Her husband motioned for her to sit back down and she returned to her seat.

Eddie took a gulp of his drink before wiping his mouth with the back of his hand. "I don't force anyone into my shops. It's entertainment."

"We can help with the marketing and all your accountancy needs," Marcus said, topping up Eddie's glass, presumably to bring the conversation back to his pitch.

"Interesting," Eddie said, unconvincingly. "I'm opening a casino next year." Eddie lifted his glass to clink it with mine. "Here's to a big future."

Fiona laughed. "The casino is a silly dream. I wish you'd sell the shops. Connor Davies offered you a small fortune for them."

Eddie threw his head back, laughing.

Tara looked over her shoulder and gave a distasteful look as Eddie's laugh turned into a smoker's cough.

"He's the last person I'd sell to," Eddie said, pointing at his wife. "You just want the cash so you can expand your stables."

"There's a lot of money in training." Fiona sipped her fizz as she studied the cutlery.

"So why's your family so broke?" Eddie said.

"Don't be crass." Fiona placed the fork back on the table.

I felt relieved to see Elena approaching.

Fiona picked up her spoon and addressed Elena. "Interesting cutlery. I'm refurbishing our Bristol apartment. I'd quite like something similar. Is it antique?"

"It belonged to my uncle," Elena said. "He brought it with him from where he worked in a London kitchen."

I wondered whether he'd pinched it because when I looked closer; I noticed it had *Pilkington Hotel* stamped into it.

As if reading my mind, Elena continued. "The hotel closed. The liquidators sold off the cutlery, and chinaware. Uncle Luigi moved over to Branden Bay as the air was cleaner and opened this bistro." She gestured around the room and smiled.

"Ah, you're Italian," Eddie said.

"I take it your waitress is new? She was ever so clumsy," Fiona said. "Maybe she's not suited to restaurant work."

I raised my eyebrows. I thought her words were mean. After all, the woman only dropped a glass.

Elena ignored Fiona's comments. "Are you ready to order?"

"I'll have a four seasons pizza." Eddie gestured at his wife. "She'll have a medium-well eight-ounce rump. Becky wants the lasagne and what do you want, Mark?" he said, looking at Marcus.

Marcus flinched. He hated it when people got his name wrong. I would have laughed under normal circumstances, but I was none too happy with Eddie Fly, who clearly thought women were unable to order food for themselves.

"Actually, Elena," I interrupted. "Could I have the fillet steak from the specials board?" As much as I adored Corelli's lasagne, there was no way I was going to let this guy speak for me.

Marcus frowned at the menu. "I've not got much of an appetite. Could I please have the Mediterranean soup with ciabatta toast?"

I raised my eyebrows. Maybe the directors of the firm had asked him to keep the costs down.

While we waited for our food to arrive, Marcus droned on about the history of the London firm. Eddie stood up and removed his jacket, ignoring Marcus's spiel, which I knew off by heart, from my years in London.

I turned away. Councillor Levison and his wife were making their way through a bottle of wine. He was red in the face and his wife was sitting with her back to me. He clocked I was looking at them and she turned around, giving me a big smile and a little wave, probably recognising me from the newspapers.

I nodded at her, then turned as the door of the restaurant banged in the wind as it shut. The blonde waitress was walking away from the restaurant with her coat over her arm. I shook my head, hoping Fiona hadn't got her the sack by highlighting her clumsiness.

What a pair, I thought, peering at the odd couple I was sitting with. Eddie also seemed to watch the waitress walk away. He leaned back and began tapping into his mobile phone.

Fiona reached for her small clutch bag. "Excuse me," she said, then rose and walked in the direction of the restroom.

As Marcus and Eddie's conversation turned to football betting, my eyes were drawn to H. Tara glanced over her shoulder and scowled. *What's her problem?* I thought. There was hatred in her eyes. *What on earth have I done to deserve a look like that? She's the one dating H*. I caught H's dark expression. I gave a small smile, which he didn't return. Sighing, I stood and made my way to the restroom. As I approached, I saw Fiona standing at the kitchen door, smiling as she waved through the porthole window.

She turned and flicked her hair as I approached. "I like to check a kitchen is clean before I eat. You can never be too careful these days." She looked over my shoulder. "Are they still droning on about business?"

I nodded. "They're discussing the profitability of premier league gambling."

"I'm not silly, you know. Marcus has only pulled you along to impress Eddie." She looked over at the table. "You clearly have no interest in marketing or moving to London." She sighed. "My husband is obsessed with celebrity. I guess Marcus thought you'd be the bait."

"Very perceptive," I said. "But I'm hardly a celebrity."

"But there's potential. You're just the sort of person the public is interested in these days. This paranormal thing could turn into something big. You could be one of those influencers. But forgive me, I think the ghost thing is utter rubbish." She flicked her hair. "Although clearly, you're a decent amateur sleuth, finding those diamonds. Can't say I would have handed them over myself." She lowered her voice. "Did you keep a sneaky few?"

I laughed. "There was a whole SWAT team breathing down my neck. I doubt I could have got away with it. And there was a reward, anyway."

"I'd better get back to the table. It's all business with Eddie. Sometimes the things you find most attractive in a person when you meet them turn out to be the things you hate about them when you're married." She moved away from me.

She'd been quite open, and that surprised me. As I passed the kitchen, I too looked in the window. I noticed a shaven-haired male chef dressed in the usual white with chequered trousers working away. I was looking forward to my food.

Once inside the ladies' room, I shook my head at my reflection. "How did you get yourself into this situation?" I asked myself aloud. Fiona had seen straight through me, but it wasn't my fault. Marcus shouldn't have lied. After washing my hands and smoothing my hair, I left the room and bumped straight into H.

"What are you doing?" he asked in the authoritative tone that always got my back up.

"Having dinner," I replied.

"Eddie Fly is not the sort of man you want to get involved with."

I glanced to the side of H, to see Tara raising her eyebrows with a small smile on her face. "Maybe you should stop worrying about what I'm doing and concentrate on your date." I crossed my arms and looked up into his eyes. I didn't mean to sound sarcastic, it just slipped out. *Why do I have to be so confrontational with him?* I asked myself.

He smiled, and I didn't need to be psychic to guess he'd clocked I was jealous. "Nice dress you're wearing," he said. "A bit more flowery than your usual style."

I gulped. I was finding it difficult to ignore the fact that I fancied him. My feelings were spilling out all over the place. "Thanks, but I was trying to look unappealing."

"You failed." He laughed. "You're unique."

I blushed hard. I needed to rein it in. "Text me when you're next free to discuss whatever it was you wanted to chat about." I'd used a cheery voice, hoping I sounded cool as I sidestepped him and went back to the table.

Marcus frowned at me as I sat down. "Was that guy you were speaking to the copper I saw earlier at your place?"

I smiled at him. "Yes. It's a small town."

We were interrupted as Elena brought our food to the table.

The meal was amazing. The sauce on my steak, which was cooked to perfection, had a garlicky, herby deliciousness which took me to another place. And the fries were spot on. Crunchy and salty.

Fiona scowled at her husband as he ate his pizza with his hands. "They provide cutlery for a reason," she said, gripping the steak knife in her hand.

"Stop it with the snobbery, woman. You make out you're posh, but your family are skint."

"At least I speak to my family," she muttered.

Eddie sat back and whipped the napkin from his collar and wiped his mouth with it. "Don't you dare, woman. I'm sick of your put-downs. I've made some-thing of myself. What have you done? You lived off Daddy and now you live off me."

Marcus and I exchanged a glance as silence fell.

I scanned the room. Everyone's eyes were fixed on Eddie, and there was not one smile between them. H glowered, Tara had a furrowed brow, Councillor Levi-son's face was crimson, his wife was staring as if watching an episode of Dynasty, and Elena turned up the piped music.

Eddie called out to her. "This food is blinding." He waved a pizza crust at her. "Can you get the chef out so I can give him my thanks?"

"No. No. No. Don't be so silly Eddie," Fiona jumped in. "I'm sure passing on a message will suffice."

Elena approached the table, clearly not wanting to

shout across the room. "I'll give him your compliments."

"I insist. Get the guy out," Eddie said with a smile at Fiona.

Elena nodded and went to the kitchen. She returned with the chef. He looked to be in his forties, had a weathered face. He was not smiling.

"Ah, Frank. I should have guessed." Eddie raised his glass. "Great grub as per usual."

Frank gave a single nod and returned to the kitchen without speaking.

"A man of few words," Eddie added with a laugh. "See you tomorrow Frank," he called after him.

"You're not funny, Eddie," Fiona said.

"Well, I hope you're paying him well," Eddie said, looking at Elena. "He owes me money on his betting account and is behind with his payments. We're having a meeting to discuss it. So he might need a raise, love," he said with a laugh.

"That's enough." Fiona turned to me. "I'm sorry. My husband doesn't know the meaning of the word 'discretion'."

"Would you like to see the dessert menu?" Elena asked, without her usual smile.

"That'd be great," Eddie said.

Elena handed out menus.

I shook my head. "Not for me, thank you." I'd had enough. The tension was mounting, it was time for me to go. I was just about to stand up when Mrs Levison rose from her seat and walked towards us. *Not another confrontation,* I thought.

"Gina, no," her husband called after her, but she made a beeline for our table.

"Hello, Eddie," she said as she approached our table.

"Gina," Eddie leaned back in his chair.

Fiona shook her head.

"How's your upward elevation in social circles going?" Eddie said. "I understand you're soon to be the mayoress of Branden Bay. Now who would have thought that?"

"I need to have a chat with you." She gave a sideways glance to Fiona. "In private."

Fiona gave a loud sigh.

"I can see you up at Millar's for breakfast if you like?" He looked over at Levison. "I'll be speaking to your husband tomorrow at eleven. Come before then."

She turned and smiled at me. "And you're that Becky James, aren't you?" Her beaming smile made up for her drab clothes.

I stifled a yawn. "Yes."

"I hear you're involved with the Victorian Town Theme Day. Hopefully, I'll see you at the planning meeting."

"Er, yeah," I said, remembering the pier owner, Andrew Farr had mentioned a meeting to me. I'd been considering excuses as to why I could not attend.

She turned back to Eddie. "I'll see you tomorrow

then, in the restaurant at ten." She made her way to the ladies' room.

We heard the scraping of a chair and Councillor Levison rose and stormed over. I frowned and was sure I recognised his voice as he near shouted at Eddie.

"Keep away from my wife."

Eddie sat back. "Levison, I told you before, Gina is strictly off limits for me. If she wasn't, she wouldn't be married to you, would she?" He threw his head back and laughed.

"Well, don't mind me." Fiona pursed her lips. "Sit down, Nigel. You're winding him up and creating a scene."

Levison spun around and returned to his table.

This was the final straw for me. The atmosphere was so thick it would have taken a chainsaw to get through it. I stood up. "Well, it's been great to meet you," I lied as I smiled at Fiona and Eddie. "But I've an early start." I turned to Marcus. "Can you see me out?" I raised my eyebrows at him.

"Of course," he said, standing up, looking more than a little nervous.

And so he should, I thought, subjecting me to such an awful evening. As I passed H, Tara spooned choco-late ice-cream into his mouth and gave me a saccharin smile. I reached for my pashmina, watching Councillor Levison stabbing his finger at his wife as she returned to their table. He fixed his eyes on Eddie, who was, yet again, arguing with Fiona.

Once outside, I turned to Marcus. "I don't know

what you're playing at, but I'm not coming to London. I don't want the job you're offering. I've wasted three years of my life trying to be what you wanted me to be. You only ever cared about yourself. You're a self-centred weasel, and I'm sorry to be the one to tell you, but the entire world does not spin around you." I took a deep breath. "Since I've been here, in Branden Bay, I've become someone new. I'm not the person I used to be."

"I can see that," he said looking at me from the top of my head right down to my purple painted toenails. "But I think you're being a bit harsh, Becks."

"Stop calling me that."

"But –"

"I don't expect to see you ever again. We're done. Goodbye, Marcus."

"Babe ..." he called out as I walked away.

I didn't look back. I'd not even one smidgen of regret for walking away from my previous world in London. Life in Branden Bay was good, more than good.

Once home, I went upstairs and found Constance asleep on my bed. I laid down, stroked her and drifted off to sleep, still in my clothes.

I WOKE SOME HOURS LATER. My hands fizzed, and static raced up to my head.

"Oh no, not again," I cried out, knowing this meant

a spirit was close by. I'd not experienced any paranormal activity for a couple of weeks and hoped that I'd started a peaceful period. I was wrong.

Constance hissed at my side, staring at the ensuite bathroom. I saw light flickering underneath the bathroom door. There was little doubt in my mind that something was lurking inside.

Constance jumped from the bed and scratched at the door. With it not being properly closed, she pushed it open. I heard someone sloshing in the bath. My heart pounded. I didn't want to go in there, but something pulled at me. Then came the sound of a man singing an old folk tune. "In Dublin's fair city, where the girls are so pretty, I first set my eyes on sweet ..." and he went on, slightly off key, accompanied by sloshing water.

I slipped off the bed, pins and needles buzzing on my bare feet as I walked across the well-worn carpet. As I reached the bathroom, the static increased with every step. I opened the door and stopped short. In my bathtub was a naked Eddie Fly.

"What are you doing?" I asked. Thinking it was him in the flesh.

He didn't respond. He lifted his thick leg and rubbed his foot with a sponge as he continued belting out the song. "... crying cockles and mussels ..."

Constance hissed, and her coat bushed out.

The vision of Eddie flickered. It was definitely not the flesh and blood Eddie. He looked in my direction;

the smile slid off his face. "What are you doing here?" He let go of his foot.

"This is my bathroom," I said. "In my house."

"I told you we'd meet tomorrow." He shook his head, then sat back and clutched the side of the bath. "Are you mad?"

I looked around the room. Eddie was the only person I could see in the vision.

"What are you doing?" He paused. "Get that knife away from me."

"What?" I said. I had nothing on me, let alone a knife.

Constance began a long, low, wailing meow.

Eddie put his hands up. "Let's be sensible about this." There was fear in his eyes, which were bulging open. "No. No. No." He screamed as he lunged his hands out towards me, splashing as he tried to get up.

I stood transfixed, and so was Constance.

As I watched him flaying around, a slither of red appeared on his neck. He clutched his throat.

I turned away. "Urgh!" I didn't want to see what was coming. I heard one last cry. Then silence fell. The only sound was of dripping water from the tap.

Constance gave a wailing meow, and I gingerly turned around. Eddie lay in a bath of red-coloured water.

I screamed. The vision disappeared, and it left me standing in darkness, as if someone had just turned the lights out. My hand shook as I pulled the light cord, but as the room became illuminated, the tub was empty and shining clean.

Jeff and Dannie burst into my bedroom.

"What's happening?" Dannie asked wrapping her dressing gown around herself. I could hear the fear in her voice.

"Is it a spirit?" Jeff asked eagerly as he stood in his Hulk underpants.

I nodded. "I need to call H. Someone's been murdered."

CHAPTER 5

"*W*hat's the matter?" H asked in a groggy voice as he answered my call. "This better be good. I've only just got to sleep."

"I need to tell you something," I said into my phone as I sat in the kitchen with Dannie who was making tea. My hands shook with static aftershock. Jeff was upstairs in my bathroom setting up his paranormal equipment.

H groaned. "We can talk about your boyfriend tomorrow."

"Sorry if I'm interrupting something," I snapped. "But it's important." I snatched a banoffee muffin from my tin of ugly cakes – the one's that never made it into the café.

H growled. "You're not interrupting anything, Becky. I'm alone."

I let out a breath. "There's been a murder."

He paused and sounded much more awake. "Are you sure?"

"Well, I think there has," I said. After all, it was a vision.

"Where are you?"

"At home."

H ARRIVED TEN MINUTES LATER. His hair was all mussed up, and I gulped, pushing somewhat inappropriate thoughts out of my mind. I handed him a coffee and offered him the cake tin. He needed to be alert.

I explained what I'd seen, as he devoured a broken flapjack.

He sat back with his coffee mug in hand. "So, let me get this straight. You've had a bad dream about a dangerous man being stabbed in the throat and killed in his bath and you've got me out of bed, so I can check with Millar's Hotel to make sure he's still alive?"

I had to admit. It did sound ridiculous. "I had static, pins and needles. You know that happens when I see a spirit."

H's expression relaxed. "Come on, then." He placed his empty mug in the sink. "I'll drive us up there."

Rain battered the kitchen window and a breeze blew under the door.

"I'll change," I said. I was still wearing the floral dress.

Upstairs in my room, I found Jeff fixing his camera onto a tripod. He used it to pick up the presence of any spiritual being, which would be displayed on the viewfinder as a stick person. "I've set it to record, so we can monitor it twenty-four seven." He glanced at his EMF meter which monitored changes in the electro-magnetic field. "It's not picking anything up yet."

"I want to clean my teeth," I said. "And I'm about to get changed, so can you give me some privacy?"

H PUT his car into gear and turned on the windscreen wipers as the rain pelted down hard. "I didn't realise you were bringing the cat."

"She followed me out." I rubbed Constance's damp fur as she sat on my lap.

"So how well do you know Eddie Fly?"

"It was the first time I'd met him."

"He's a nasty piece of work. He's been on Brad's radar for a while."

I groaned. Brad was also known as award-winning D.C.I. Bradley Harris and was on Avon and Somerset's vice squad. He only did bad cop and was far from fond of me, after I'd got myself mixed up in the middle of one of his investigations.

H drove along Beach Road. "I'm sure Fly's still alive, but if we find him dead, Brad'll be all over it."

I groaned.

"He's probably fine. Having dinner with Fly is enough to give anyone nightmares." H laughed.

I hoped he was right. "Marcus had invited me to the meal hoping my so-called 'celebrity' would help persuade Eddie to take his business to the London accountancy firm he works at."

"From the way the guy spoke in your garden, it was like you still had a long-distance relationship."

"We worked together, and we lived together. It didn't work out. I moved here. That's it. I just wanted to erase him from my mind. I wasn't hiding anything if it came across that way. I've made it crystal clear to Marcus. I never want to set eyes on him again."

H caught my eye and smiled. "It's not surprising he wants you back. He was an idiot to let you go."

I gulped. Was H suggesting I was a real catch? "That's Marcus for you," I said in a high-pitched voice as H reached the end of the prom. "So, how's it going with Tara?" I asked as he turned up the road to Millar's. Ahead of us, outside of the hotel, was an ambulance and police car.

I swallowed hard and grabbed his arm.

"Calm down. It's probably a co-incidence." H drove up close then killed the engine, and the wipers stopped. He patted my hand, which was still clutching his bicep, and I felt a fizz run up my arm. I moved to get out of the car.

"No, you stay here with your cat." He passed me the car keys. "Lock yourself in."

Constance meowed in protest as H exited and I pressed the lock door button on the dash.

I scratched Constance's head as she stared out of the front window, which was filled with rainwater. Dread sloshed all over me, I didn't believe in coincidence. I saw movement out the side of my eye, peering through the droplets on the window, I noticed a woman in a coat step onto the street from a shop doorway with her hood up. I looked front as another police car drew up and parked behind us. They jumped out of their vehicle and ran into the hotel. When I looked around, the woman had gone.

"I can't just sit here, Connie cat. I need to know what's going on."

Constance meowed as if she agreed.

"Come on then, but you'll have to be good." I got out and took the keys which H had left with me. After locking the car, I ran the short distance to the entrance as the puddles wet the bottoms of my jeans.

I walked inside the hotel lobby with Constance under my arm. It was quiet. No security guard was at the desk, or any police. I took the stairs, deciding to check each floor as I went. All was quiet on the first, second, and third floors. I panted as I reached the fourth and heard voices. Out of the stairwell I found hotel guests wearing their nightwear, in the corridor. They fell silent as we heard Fiona's wailing voice. "I told him not to push buttons. I can't believe it."

"What's going on?" I asked a man close to me.

"There were screams. We all came out. I think someone's dead."

I shut my eyes. I'd been right. I opened them to the sound of H's voice. I could not see him so peeked around the female guest standing in front of me, while shielding myself from his view.

"Can I have your attention, please? This is police business. We will create an incident room at the hotel. We will inform you of its location and you will be required to make a full statement before you leave. Failure to do so will involve you returning to Branden Bay at a future date for questioning. Please now return to your rooms."

Behind him a paramedic led a blanket-covered Fiona down the corridor. "We'll find a quiet room for you, Mrs Fly."

After the guests went inside their rooms and Fiona and the paramedic took the lift, there was just me left standing by the door to the stairway with Constance at my feet, staring at police taping the entrance to the room.

H approached me. "I said to wait in the car."

I put a hand to my neck. "He's dead, isn't he?"

Constance gave a low, wailing meow.

H put a hand on my shoulder as he reached me. "Yes. And there's something else you need to know." His expression darkened. "Someone saw your ex at the hotel."

"Marcus?" I asked.

He nodded. "What's his surname?"

"Day." I shook my head. "But he's staying here. So, it's no surprise that he was spotted."

"Do you know what room he's in?"

"No. You don't honestly see him as a suspect, do you?"

"At the moment, he's a person of interest."

"There's no way Marcus would kill." I pointed toward the taped room.

H took a step back. "I know it's difficult to comprehend. But maybe you didn't know him as well as you thought. People change."

I frowned. "He won't have changed into a killer in a few short months."

"For every murderer, there are at least three people who say they can't believe it. They were such a nice, well-adjusted person. Murderers take many forms."

"No." I shook my head. "He's too squeamish to stab someone in the neck."

H took his phone out of his pocket. "I need his mobile number."

"I blocked him and deleted it from my phone."

He raised his eyebrows at me. "This is a guy you lived with for years. You must know it off by heart. Come on," he growled at me.

It was true; I knew it. But I still hesitated.

"Look, if he's innocent, there isn't a problem, is there?" H said. "He needs to be discounted. He'll continue to be a suspect until we satisfy ourselves that he had nothing to do with it."

"I think I know it," I said before reeling off the number which had been etched into my memory.

"I'll drive you home," H said after he noted the number.

I handed him the car keys. "No, it's alright. You're busy. I'll call Jeff to come and get me."

"No snooping around," H said as I entered the stairwell.

I didn't call Jeff for a ride. The rain had stopped, so I walked back because it was not that much of a journey and I wanted to clear my head. I contemplated calling Marcus, but decided I was best out of it. As I rounded the bend of the road onto the seafront, I clutched Constance close to my chest as the sea breeze blew and the rain returned.

How can Marcus be the prime suspect? I thought, wiping the dampening hair from my face. It was ludicrous, just because he was staying at the same hotel, it didn't make him a murderer.

Ten minutes later, I walked up to my front door. Constance hissed, and I stopped dead. *Please don't let it be the spirit of Eddie Fly.*

"Becks."

I turned around. Marcus was crouched on my patio, hiding behind the wall, his rain drenched hair stuck to his face. "You've got to help me. Eddie's dead and I've just had a call from the police. I let it go to voicemail, and when I listened to the message, they said they want me to help them with their enquiries." He stood up and approached me.

I squeezed Constance against my chest to prevent her from attacking him. "How do you know Eddie's dead?" My blood ran cold. *Could Marcus have done it?*

He hugged himself. "I saw him, with my own eyes, lying dead in his bath. I've been down the seafront, puking my guts up. Then I knocked on your door and a girl answered and said you were out. I was just sitting here, wondering what to do next, when you showed up."

I nodded at him as Constance struggled and meowed. "Get to Millar's now. If you're innocent, you've nothing to worry about," I said. I wanted Marcus as far away from my place as possible. I didn't want to get involved. "They're up there now, trying to find out what room you're in."

"Let's go inside. The rain's getting harder," he said.

"No way. You need to sort this out."

He came towards me, dodging a swipe from Constance. "I'm staying at the Budget Inn. I said I was up at Millar's to impress you." He put his hands to his forehead. "This is serious. I'm scared, Becks."

"So, if you weren't staying at Millar's, what were you doing in Eddie's room?"

"I – "

The sound of a car approaching interrupted Marcus. It was H. I groaned as I watched him screech to a stop outside my house.

Marcus took a few steps to my door, sheltering behind me as if he was four years old. It didn't really work, seeing as he's a good foot taller than me.

H jumped out, gesturing at me. "When were you going to tell me he was here?"

"I've only just got back," I said.

Constance jumped to the floor and sashayed over to H, rubbing up against his legs as if to say it was absolutely nothing to do with her.

I put my hands on my hips as the rain came down harder. "Marcus was just about to call you." I blinked a rain drop from my eye.

A police car approached with the lights flashing. It stopped and two officers got out. Marcus walked around me with his hands up, as if the police were armed.

H shook his head as he picked up Constance and passed her back to me. "Get inside your house, you're getting drenched. I'll speak to you later."

Dannie opened the door. "I saw lights flashing from my bedroom window. What's going on? Some crazy guy with staring eyes knocked on asking for you earlier."

"That was Marcus." I pointed to him getting into a police car. "He wasn't at his best. He was frightened." I walked in the house as the police drove off, shaking from both the chilly rain and the situation.

Constance jumped from me and into the hall and I followed her. "Eddie was indeed murdered, and Marcus appears to be the prime suspect." I sighed. "He was up at Millar's, found the body and, rather than reporting it to the police, the idiot fled the scene."

"Do you think he did it?" Dannie asked as she closed the front door.

"No, but the police do," I said.

"Jeff's upstairs, still in your room. Do you want a cup of tea?"

I shook my head. "No, I'm going to have a hot shower and get some sleep."

After showering in the family bathroom, I found Jeff asleep on the floor of my room. *Brilliant, just brilliant.* I pulled my PJs on and slipped into bed, falling into a restless sleep.

My alarm went off as it always did at six. I woke with a sick feeling inside my stomach. I looked across to the rug to see Jeff still sleeping, in the foetal position cuddling his EMF meter like it was a teddy bear. The alarm had not woken him. Beyond him was his paranormal set up in the open door of the en suite. I grabbed some clothes for the day and took them to the family bathroom.

In the kitchen, I whizzed up batter in a commercial mixer I'd bought. "No doubt Bad Cop Brad, will be on the case and have me in for questioning," I said to Constance as she ate her fishy breakfast.

She gave a low meow. She wasn't keen on him either.

I was baking my favourite Victoria sponge and a batch of scones, deciding to do 'all day afternoon tea'. It was the quickest option as I needed time to work on my statement, and it also reminded me of Grandma, and I found that comforting. I smiled at Constance. I always felt Grandma was close by when Constance was near me. Maybe it was because I'd named her after her. I guessed as a medium I could learn to call Grandma up, but I had no intention of developing my gift. All I wanted to do was to cope with it.

As I filled my dishwasher, I glanced at the clock, wondering whether Marcus was still being questioned. I took a deep breath, he was nothing to do with me anymore and it wasn't my problem that he'd got himself into this situation.

After removing the last of my bakes from the oven, I jumped as there was a knock at the back door. I unlocked it to find Lynn on the doorstep.

"Lovey, I felt it in my bones. Something's up. Are you okay? Was it that Marcus fella?"

I grabbed Lynn for a hug, then explained what had happened. Her eyes grew wide as I described seeing Eddie in my bathtub. Constance added meows and hisses, as if backing up my story.

Lynn waggled her index finger at me. "Now forget about running away from your gift. You need to get this one nipped in the bud, lovey. We'll do a séance tonight."

Constance hissed but rubbed up against Lynn as if in agreement.

I was going to protest, but Lynn had a point. I needed to communicate with Eddie, ask who killed him, and simply pass the name over to the police. I shuddered. I really hoped it wasn't Marcus. Did I really know him as well as I thought I did?

"A séance?" Dannie stood in the kitchen doorway, fresh out of bed. "You said you'd never do that?"

"It'll be the quickest way to solve his murder," I said. "Instead of going around the houses."

"I think I'll go out this evening," Dannie said as she walked away, tapping into her phone.

"I don't blame you," I said. "What time will we do it?" I asked Lynn.

"About half nine, when it's dark. It's easier to concentrate in the evening and town is quieter."

The café phone rang.

"Connie's café." Dannie answered it in the hall.

I pulled a chair out and sat at the kitchen table, hoping the call wasn't the police requesting my presence.

Dannie returned. "It's for you," she said, passing me the handset for the landline. "It's Marcus," she said.

Constance gave a low growl.

I huffed and took the phone and spoke into it. "Have they let you out?"

"They said I could make one call."

"I think you should call a lawyer."

"I can't afford one, Becks. Can you come in?"

No, no, no. I said in my mind.

"Are you still there?" Marcus asked.

"I have buttercream to make," I replied.

"Please, you're my only hope."

I paused. I wanted to refuse with every part of my being, but heard myself say, "See you in half an hour."

CHAPTER 6

"*Y*ou've got to help me, Becks," Marcus said across the interview room table at the police station.

I tutted. "You need a professional."

"You've found killers and recovered stolen jewels. I don't need a lawyer. That won't work. They don't know me like you do, they'll just think I did it and make some sort of deal. I need you to find the actual killer to get the police off my back."

The policeman guarding the door with his arms crossed, slowly shook his head.

"I'm not a detective but H, I mean Sergeant Blake, is great. I'm sure he'll find the truth."

"He doesn't like me, I can tell."

Hmmm, I thought, *He's a lot better than D.C.I. Brad Harris.* Hopefully, Bad Cop Brad would leave this case to H.

"Please, Becky. Don't you want to help me? We have history."

I sighed, wanting to walk out, to forget the whole thing and never see Marcus again. But a trickle of curiosity seeped into my veins. I pulled my smartphone from my bag to make notes. "Tell me, what were you doing at Millar's hotel? Seeing as you weren't staying there. What's going on?"

Marcus looked at his hands. "They let me go."

"Who?"

"The firm, after I took Juliet on."

"I presume you're referring to the woman who took the job you'd promised me for years?"

He nodded. "They told me they needed to cut back on middle management and Juliet is now doing what I did for half the salary and they gave me a paltry pay-off."

"Middle management? You're a director."

"I was an associate director, on the board, but not a shareholder."

"Surely you can find another job with your experience?"

He shook his head. "Not for anything like that money. I'd have to start again. I thought if I could get Eddie Fly's business, what with the shops he has all over the country, it would be a huge account. I thought they'd take me back." He looked up at me. "And I could have negotiated a position for you as well. I had it all planned out. We'd have made a great team. But I messed up. I've lost you and my career."

I ignored his pitiful expression. "So, what were you doing up at the hotel after the meal?"

"I told Eddie I was staying there, I didn't want to say I was at the Budget Inn. So I walked back with them." He shook his head. "They argued all the way."

"What about?"

"She was accusing him of still being in love with his ex and he was accusing her of sleeping around. When we reached the hotel, he shut it down. Said he wanted a divorce and told her to move out of their Bristol apartment and go to their country home. He said he'd talk about the separation the next day and muttered something about a top lawyer. I waited for Fiona to go up and then I asked Fly when we could discuss him moving his business to us and he told me he had enough to contend with, that he'd contact me after his separation went through. That could have taken months."

"Or years," I added.

"I couldn't wait. I guess he just wanted a free meal with you, the local celebrity, while in town. That restaurant bill blew me out."

"So, why did you go to his room?"

"I was desperate, I'd sat at the bar drinking a coffee, which I was literally fumbling for coins to pay for, when I saw Fiona come down. She ordered a coffee to go and asked them to charge it to room 403. I wanted another chat with Eddie. I thought he just needed to calm down a bit after his argument with Fiona." He shook his head. "She sat with me chatting about blinking horses as cool as you like, as if the huge argument had never happened. And then, once her coffee was ready, she left. I took it as my opportunity, so I slipped up the stairs. And then when I got there." He paused, then looked into my eyes. "It was awful Becks. You don't know what I saw."

I knew exactly but would not discuss my vision with him. "Why did you feel desperate enough to go into a potential clients' hotel room late in the evening?"

"I've nothing to lose. I'm broke. I don't even have enough for the train fare home."

"Your apartment must be worth a small fortune. I heard that Thameside properties sell immediately. Put it on the market, Marcus. Prices have skyrocketed, it's going to be worth a couple of million at least."

He sighed without comment.

"Have you mortgaged it up to the max?" I asked.

He shook his head. "I rented it off one of the directors at the firm."

"You told me you owned it."

"I wanted to impress you." He looked at me and reached his hand across the table.

"No touching," called the police officer from the door.

Suits me. I sat back in my seat and put my hands on my lap. "I wouldn't have cared, Marcus."

"The rent is punishing. That's why we never did much. I'd have loved to have taken you away. Maybe when this nightmare is over, we can go on holiday somewhere in the Mediterranean. I can pay you back for my half of the trip when I'm back on my feet."

The policeman glanced at me and gave a silent tut. His reaction was spot on. Marcus was delusional. The last thing I was going to do was jet off with him on a romantic getaway. And he expected me to pay!

Marcus ran a hand through his messy hair. "I've got one week left, then I have to move out. They said they're going to send my stuff over to my parents if I don't clear it out." He put his head in his hands. "They'll be so ashamed."

I wanted to get the conversation away from Marcus and back to the murder. "What time did you go to the hotel?"

He lifted his head from his arms. "I guess we got there at about ten forty-five. So it was probably well gone eleven when I found him dead."

"He let you in?"

"No. I knocked on the door and it pushed open. I went in and found him lying in a bath of blood. His eyes were staring at me." Marcus put his hand to his throat. "It was awful."

I was having flashbacks.

"After seeing that, I ran. I slipped over on some sort of necklace made of beads."

"A necklace?"

"Yeah, it looked like one of those religious ones."

"A rosary?" I asked.

He nodded. "I fell to the floor, picked myself up and scarpered."

"Why didn't you call the police? If you'd gone straight to reception, you wouldn't have looked so guilty."

"Eddie Fly has a reputation for shady dealings. I didn't want to get on the wrong side of his enemies. I presumed it was a hit and didn't want my name mixed up with it all, they might've knocked me off too."

I shook my head. "Eddie Fly is caught up in that scene? And he's someone you want as a client?"

"Trust me, a lot of the clients at the London firm are bad news. It never stopped us from taking them on. Crooks still have to pay tax, you know. Well, some tax, sometimes. That's our job to limit the liability."

I let a long breath out, pleased I was no longer involved with a company like that.

"Right, that's your time up." The policeman moved towards us.

"Becks, help me."

"Marcus, how can I help when you've just admitted to lying to me for years? I don't even know you." I stood up. "As I said earlier, get yourself a lawyer." I walked towards the door, then called over my shoulder. "Good luck."

Once in the corridor, I made my way to the exit. As I walked out, H appeared. "Wait. Come back inside, I need to go over what you saw in your dream."

I put my hands on my hips. "It wasn't a dream." I hadn't meant to snap at him. Marcus had wound me up, and I was still feeling the effects. I followed H into a different interview room.

"So, the dream. What happened step by step?" He motioned for me to sit down. "Last night you told me you'd seen Eddie with his throat cut. Did you see anything before that?"

"He was in the bath." I sat down. "He said something like, 'What are you doing here? No, no stop, get that away from me.' Then I saw a line of red on his throat so looked away. He cried out. When I turned back, the bathwater had turned red. He was laying in it. Then the vision disappeared."

"Did he mention any names?"

"No. But it was clearly someone he knew because he had said he would discuss whatever the person had come in about the following day. So it was someone he planned to meet today."

"And likely to be someone who fled the scene in a hurry. Your boyfriend ticks the boxes."

"Ex-boyfriend," I said. "And Eddie wasn't planning on meeting Marcus."

"Says who?"

"Marcus but ..."

"And let's be real. We're discussing a dream, not a factual event."

I stood up. "In that case, there's no need for me to discuss it with you." I gestured towards the door. "When are you releasing Marcus? You've nothing on him, have you? Apart from the fact that he was at the hotel. Everyone knows the usual suspect is the spouse."

"It was Fiona that found Eddie."

"She was supposedly going back to Bristol and Marcus saw her leave. Why was she back?"

"She'd picked up the shop keys by mistake, so went back to get her house keys."

"Convenient."

H sat back in his chair. "Mrs Fly saw your boyfriend making a sharp exit down the stairs when she got out of the lift. Then proceeded to the hotel room, found the door open and Eddie in the bath dead. As your ex-boyfriend fled the scene, he is our prime suspect." He paused. "Why would he run? Rather than alert the police?"

"He freaked out when he saw the body, he thought it was a professional hit."

"A hit? Maybe one he arranged?"

"Of course not. He was afraid the killer would turn on him."

"There's CCTV in the lobby and the comings and goings corroborate with Mrs Fly's story."

"Maybe she snuck in and out of the fire escape to kill him and then came around the front to put the blame on someone else. Who else is on the CCTV? Is there CCTV on the fire escape or the back route? Is there CCTV on corridors of the hotel?"

"That's not your concern."

"It is if I'm representing Marcus." I folded my arms, wondering what on earth I was saying, considering I'd just told Marcus to sort out his own mess.

"Representing him?" H laughed. "One minute you are an amateur sleuth, now you're an amateur lawyer?"

"Check out his wife. They were arguing in the restaurant and on the walk back, he asked her for a divorce. Surely you witnessed they were on far from good terms. Or were you too engrossed with Tara?" I spat her name out and thrust my hands by my side.

H paused, giving me a glimmer of a smile. I felt myself heat up, and a blush crept up my neck.

He leaned forward. "We're focusing on your date last night, not mine." He looked down at his notebook. "Sit down, I need as much information about Marcus Day as you can give me. Mrs Fly will, of course, be questioned, but you're not here to discuss her. This is informal. I can bring another officer in and make this official and I'm not saying that won't happen, because a man has died. I want his history. Now."

I took a deep breath and sat in the chair with a long exhale, I appreciated H would need background on Marcus. I told him everything I knew about my ex and relayed all the details about my earlier conversation with him. When I left, I felt drained and after giving him details of my previous relationship with Marcus, I felt foolish and immature, not the sort of person any man would want to have a date with, let alone strike up a relationship. I'd laid myself bare and H had said nothing. He probably felt like he'd had a lucky escape.

$\mathcal{I}$ felt much better following my shift at the café. Admittedly, with grey skies and constant rain, we were quiet, but it was nice to have only a few locals in. I tried to put Marcus and murder out of my mind and concentrate on my new life. After all, this had nothing to do with me at all, he'd got himself into this position and I needed to keep my distance. The only thing I intended to do was the séance, because I really didn't want to have Eddie's spirit lurking in my bathroom. Hopefully between them, Lynn and Jeff could zap him. If we found out who murdered him, that would be handy, but not my primary motive. I was too close to this case and didn't want to get involved. H was more than capable, and I intended to leave it all to him.

After we'd closed up and Lynn had left, I sat down in the empty café with a cappuccino. Jeff and Dannie had offered to cook dinner and I heard their raised voices from the kitchen, arguing over whether or not to put tomatoes in the fish pie. I shut the inner door, so I didn't have to listen to them. I set a table for our meal as Constance rubbed around my legs. There was a rap on the café doors, I turned around and outside were two very familiar and welcome faces.

It was my friends Izzy and Annie. I rushed to open the door. "Thank goodness you're here," I said as they both hugged me. A lump formed in my throat and tears stung my eyes.

"Hey, let us inside," Annie said. "I didn't think you'd miss us that much."

I let them pass and pulled the doors closed.

"Is everything okay?" Annie asked.

I nodded, attempting to compose myself so I was in a fit state to update them. "How was London?" I croaked.

"Darling, it was amazing," Izzy said. She was looking her usual perfect self, gliding around the café like a swan with her neat blonde bob. "I've made some great contacts. I might leave the Gazette and go freelance. I could really get my name out there in the journalistic world. And I showed Annie the sights."

"Izzy's a great tour guide. It's a shame you couldn't join us."

"I wish I'd gone. I've got myself into an awful mess while you've been away."

"Don't tell me you're involved with this Eddie Fly murder?" Annie groaned.

I nodded.

"Darling, pop the coffee machine on. Tell us all about it." Izzy's eyes shone as she pulled her notepad from her shoulder bag, no doubt hoping for another exclusive.

After telling Izzy and Annie all about it, they decided they wanted in on the séance. Jeff and Dannie stretched dinner to five portions, and we all ate a very nice fish pie made with salmon fillets and cod. It seemed Dannie had won out, as we had roasted tomatoes on the side.

After we'd cleared away the dishes and Dannie had left, Lynn appeared at the back door.

"Where are we going to carry the séance out?" I asked her.

"In your bedroom, if that is okay? As that's where you saw the spirit and Jeff already has his equipment up there," she said.

We lugged chairs up the stairs and once inside the room, Lynn told us to sit in a circle with me positioned closest to the open bathroom door. Constance perched herself on the side of the bathtub. Lynn began with a prayer of protection as we sat holding hands.

"Eddie Fly, are you there?" Lynn called out.

We waited. Nothing happened.

"Eddie, we would like to help you," she said.

No reply came.

The EMF metre showed no unexpected change in the electromagnetic field. Nothing unusual appeared on the SLS camera.

"Maybe I didn't see him and imagined it?" I said.

"It's too much of a coincidence. But it could be something else," Lynn trailed off.

"What, like Becky, had a premonition?" Izzy asked eagerly.

"Maybe. Or ..."

"What?" Annie asked.

"If he'd done something terrible ..." Lynn said.

"He could be in hell?" Annie whispered.

Constance hissed.

"He would be in a dark place, repenting," Lynn said. "Facing up to his demons and not contactable for some time."

"But I saw him in my bath," I said.

"Maybe we should try again tomorrow," Jeff said.

I looked at the bedside clock. It was gone ten.

"Come on, then girls, let's leave Becky in peace." Lynn gestured at Jeff. "And you too."

"I'm recording," he said.

"Nothing has come up," I said. "I'd prefer it if you'd take it back to your room."

Reluctantly, Jeff packed down the equipment. I bade my friends farewell, and after washing, I went to bed falling asleep as soon as my head hit the pillow.

I woke startled, full of static with Constance wailing in my ear. "Not again," I said aloud as I saw light appear under the bathroom door.

Constance hissed, and I followed her.

I banged on the bedroom wall. "Jeff," I called out. "It's happening."

He appeared in no time with the EMF metre and his mobile phone, which had a ghost hunting app on it.

"He's in there again," I said, pointing and walked towards the door.

Constance hissed.

"I can't see anything, boss," Jeff said, but the EMF meter was picking up the change in the electromagnetic field.

"I can see light under the door," I said. "And hear him sloshing in the bath."

"Go on, open it," Jeff said, his eyes bulging in anticipation.

Constance nudged the door with her nose, and it creaked open.

My heart pounded as I entered the bathroom. Eddie was in the tub again, singing. I looked closer. "He's smiling, like the cat who's got the cream. And singing that song ... *In Dublin's fair city, where the girls are so pretty* ..." Pins and needles buzzed down my back.

"Cockles and Mussels," Jeff said. "We used to sing that at school."

"Eddie, can you see me?" I asked. I turned to Jeff. "I don't think he knows I'm here. He's washing his foot again," I said, averting my eyes so I saw nothing inappropriate.

Constance hissed.

I looked back at the vision.

Eddie stared in my direction as if in shock. "What are you doing here?"

I updated Jeff on what he'd said. "He's speaking to someone and telling them that he was going to meet to them the next day and is asking if they're mad. He doesn't look happy anymore."

"What are you doing? Get that knife away from me?" Eddie cried out.

"He's looking really frightened. I think the person's going at him with the knife." I wanted to look away but had to gather as much detail as I could. "He's putting his hands up. He's petrified."

"No. No. No." Eddie screamed. I covered my eyes but called out to him. "Eddie, Eddie Fly. Who has done this to you?"

I heard a gurgling sound and peeped between my fingers. "The bathwater's turned red." It fell dark, and the vision was gone.

I puffed out and switched on the light, my hand shaking as the static dissipated. "It was exactly the same as last time," I said to Jeff. "A repeat. He doesn't see me at all so I can't communicate with him. I need to write down what he said."

"No need for that I videoed the whole thing as you repeated what he said. It's weird though," Jeff said. "The EMF meter picked up the energy, but the app never showed up a spirit. I don't get it."

I looked at my bedside clock. "It's the same time as

last night. Eleven thirty-five. Now, I must get some sleep," I said as the spasms of electricity calmed.

CONSIDERING THE INTERRUPTED SLEEP, I felt fresh the following day. Yes, in the back of my mind was the thought that Marcus was in town and I had a spirit in my bath, but I pushed that aside. The weather had turned, and it was a warm sunny day and well into the kids' school holidays. I was busy and in my happy place, selling my bakes to not only the locals, but to day trippers.

I took a couple of orders and then heard someone call my name.

"Becky, love." It was Carol, H's Mum. "How are you?" She was a pretty woman with chin-length dark hair with a shock of blonde in the fringe and the warm brown eyes that her son had inherited.

I nodded at her. "Great, thanks."

"Are you sure? Henry told me they arrested someone for the murder of that Eddie Fly. And Gail up at the Ladies Society said it was an ex-boyfriend of yours? Someone called Marcus Day."

"Word's got around then," I said. "But no, he didn't do it." I walked around the counter and gave her a hug.

"And I'm so sorry about Henry spending time with that awful woman when he should be with you."

I laughed. "I've told you many times, we were not dating, we're just friends. And I'm sure Tara is lovely."

"She's not you. Now, I want you over at mine this Sunday at one, for a roast."

"I'd love that." I released her from the hug. "Now what can I get you? It's on the house."

I sat with Carol as she ate her favourite ginger cake with English breakfast tea. I briefly filled her in on Marcus.

"So, this ex of yours is still in custody?"

I nodded. "Hopefully they'll be able to eliminate him, and he can get back to London. I'm certain he didn't kill Eddie Fly. He'd hate to get his hands dirty and has no motive. Now that Eddie's dead, Marcus's career will be six feet under too."

"Well, you know this Marcus better than anyone love. My Henry is a good policeman. Assuming Marcus is innocent, I'm sure Henry will eliminate him from his enquiries." She stood up and grabbed her handbag. "See you on Sunday, love."

CHAPTER 8

*I*t was Friday, Jeff's birthday. I shut the café early to prepare for his party and yawned – I'd had yet another interrupted night's sleep. This time I refrained from going into the en-suite bathroom and had lain in bed, with my head underneath a pillow, as Constance hissed and gave low meows.

In the kitchen, Lynn removed a batch of sausage rolls from the oven. "These look scrummylicious, lovey."

"I'm glad I made them up in advance," I said looking at the pile of food, as I stretched out my back. I'd been shifting café tables against the walls, to allow mingling room.

"It's going to be marvellous, having a buffet and music," Lynn said. "And the cake you've made for him is amazing."

I smiled as I looked at it. I'd created a figure out of

fondant to look like Jeff and added a superhero cape. "I hope he likes it."

"Well, he does think he's your gatekeeper," she chuckled. "That's a kind of superhero."

I looked out of the window and saw Constance sitting on the bench under the branches of the apple tree, her fur fluffing out in the wind.

"Where's Jeff?" Lynn asked.

"Annie's taken him for a pre-party drink at the Branden Arms, he thinks he's coming back for a small meal with the gang."

There was a knock at my front door. *Someone's early*, I thought. "I'll get it," I called out to Lynn. As I opened the door my shoulders drooped. "Marcus."

"Becks, it was awful in there. I can't wait to jump in the shower." He looked dishevelled with his usually perfectly-styled hair all messy.

"Hey, you're not coming in here," I said as I put my hand on the door frame to block the entrance.

"I've nowhere else to go." He stood with a leather holdall in his hand.

"I'm having a party for my friend Jeff. It's his twenty-first."

"That'll be nice. It'll be great to meet your new mates."

"You'll have to go back to the Budget Inn."

"When I got there, they'd packed my stuff." He lifted the bag. "The police had been over asking questions. Everyone in this town seems to know about it.

The manager said she didn't want to put customers off with me as a guest. Huh, whatever happened to innocent until proven guilty?"

"Go back to London then, the last train from Bristol is at nine. You've plenty of time to get a connection over there. Or to be sure, just call a cab. Here," I said reaching for my bag, which I kept on the hall table. I handed over forty pounds. "This should cover the journey to Bristol."

"I've been told by the police not to leave town," he said but still took the cash.

"You're joking." I put my hands on my hips.

"To give that detective you're friends with his due, he was really keen for me to leave, but some guy came in just as he was going to release me. Evil bloke, stocky. Looked more like a thug than a copper, even had a snake tattoo on his neck. He made me go through the whole story again and said I had to stay in town."

I groaned. It sounded to me as if Bad Cop Brad was on the case. "You can't stay here. I've already got a house full of lodgers." That wasn't completely true there was another spare room, the one Dannie had stayed in and a huge attic space, but I wasn't about to offer accommodation to him.

"I can bunk in with you."

"No, you can't!"

Mrs Jessup walked down her path. "Hi Becky, dear, do you want me to bring anything to the party tonight?"

I pulled Marcus in and out of sight. "Just bring what you're drinking, Mrs Jessup. See you at half seven," I said as I closed the door with Marcus inside. As much as I hated him in my house, I didn't want my neighbours to witness a scene between us.

Marcus rubbed his hands together. "So, when's the party start?"

"You're not invited. Go up to the first room at the top of the stairs." I directed him to my bedroom. "Use the shower and keep yourself out of the way. There's a TV in there. I'll bring you up a plate of food in an hour. We'll talk about this when everyone has gone home."

"Thanks Becks, you're a life saver." He climbed the stairs.

"And Marcus," I called. "Don't come down tonight or you're out."

"Okay," he grinned.

"I mean it."

"I get it." He turned and continued up the stairs.

I watched him go, thinking this was a bad idea when I heard the cat flap bang in the wind. "You'd better get up there quick because the cat's coming." I turned around to find Constance staring at me. I walked towards her and picked her up. "You're going to have to restrain yourself. I'll get rid of him as soon as I can."

THE PARTY WAS in full swing, most of the gang were there. Annie, Lynn, Izzy and Dannie and a bunch of

Jeff's work colleagues, and a few of his ghost-hunting friends that we'd managed to contact behind his back. Mrs Jessup had brought her friend and Katherine from the pier had come along with Andrew of the funfair. Constance was flirting with everyone and getting an awful lot of attention. I had tried locking her in the snug, but she'd meowed so loudly I could hear her above the music. It seemed Constance enjoyed a party as much as the grandma I'd named her after.

"Thanks, boss," Jeff said, giving me an awkward hug.

I laughed. "It's your twenty-first, we couldn't let it go without a proper celebration."

"Well, it's better than bingo last night," he laughed.

Annie danced over to me smiling. "It's a great party. We should do this for all our birthdays."

It was indeed fun, but there was one person missing, but I could forgive him. After all, he was involved in a murder investigation. I heard the doorbell ring at just before ten.

"I'll get it," Lynn walked out of the café to answer the front door. Then appeared with H behind her. "Watch out, the police are here to shut this raucous party down," Lynn said with a laugh.

I smiled and walked to greet H, noticing with relief that he'd decided to leave his girlfriend at home.

"He's on his own," Annie whispered in my ear. "Time to make a move."

"Annie," I said. "Stop stirring." Although I felt an

urge for us to have that *chat,* he'd wanted and with a couple of glasses of fizz inside me, I felt relaxed enough to be honest with him about my feelings.

"Hey, it's not stirring, it's a gentle nudge," Annie said. "Honestly, he isn't into Tara. I've known him for years and can tell. The way he looks at you is just like the way he used to look at ..." She trailed off and moved away. I knew she was referring to H's first girl-friend, Zoe, who died when they were all sixteen.

"Where's the birthday boy?" H asked as he reached me.

I pointed to Jeff knocking back a shot of something alcoholic as his friends cheered on.

H laughed. "Someone's going to have a sore head tomorrow."

"He booked the day off work," I said. "Where's Tara?"

"She already had something on in Bristol. She sends her apologies. She's really keen to get to know you better. She's thinking of moving to Branden Bay, rather than commuting every day."

"Nice," I said, not meaning it.

"She wants a fresh start. It'd be nice if you could show her around at some point."

"Me? I've only lived here a few months."

"You've been visiting this town regularly your whole life."

It was true, but I didn't add anything extra to the conversation.

"Darling," Izzy said giving H an air kiss. "Let me have a pic." She lifted her phone. "I'm doing a collection for Jeff because I forgot to buy him a gift. I'm planning to make one of those photo books for him."

"Great idea," I said.

"Well scooch up together then, you two."

I narrowed my eyes at Izzy. *I know her game,* I thought.

I lifted myself on tiptoe as H stood next to me. He put his arm around me and I felt a fizz in my body which was nothing to do with ghosts and gulped.

"Smile then. Stop looking so awkward. It looks like a school prom pic."

"Hello down there," H said.

I looked up at him and laughed. Us standing side by side for a picture was never going to work.

Izzy took a couple of shots then looked at the screen on her phone. "Beautiful, gorgeous together."

I moved to the side. "I have to bring the birthday cake through." Looking back, I saw H staring after me, he smiled. Constance jumped onto the table beside him, begging him for a stroke. I turned my head and headed for the kitchen.

"Are you okay, sweetie?" Izzy asked as she followed me in.

"Yes, why?"

"Oh come on. We all know that you and H should be together."

"He's dating Tara," I said.

"They went on a couple of dates, darling. It's not serious."

My friends seemed to see things differently to me. My mind flashed back to a vision of Corelli's, with Tara seductively shovelling chocolate ice-cream into H's mouth.

"I've captured it perfectly in the picture, I'll ping it over to you," Izzy said.

"I'm not into romance. I've got enough to worry about with Marcus here."

"He's still in Branden Bay?"

"I mean here, as in upstairs."

"What? Really?"

"It's a long story." I grabbed the cake. "Let's do the candles."

I walked into the café and stopped dead. Marcus was in the middle of the room, barefoot, wearing the purple velvet dressing gown I'd inherited from Grandma and carrying an empty plate. "Any chance of seconds, Becks?" He looked at H and then back to me. "You couldn't make me a brew, could you? You know my favourite."

I heard a hiss. I thrust the cake into H's hands and dived across the room to catch Constance, to prevent her from sinking her teeth into Marcus's bare calf. I caught her but slipped, ending up flat on the floor and skidded until I slammed against the sideboard as a plastic bowl of crisps rained down on me. I looked up with Constance wriggling in my arms, H stared down at us with his mouth agape.

"Here," Lynn said as she grabbed my wriggling cat.

I tried pulling myself up from the floor as ladylike as I could. H couldn't help me up as he held the cake but Marcus moved forward and tugged my arm.

As soon as I was upright, I yanked back my hand and brushed crisps from my hair. "What part of *stay upstairs* did you not understand?" I hissed at my unwanted guest.

I turned to H, he said nothing, but his eyes told me his thoughts.

"Marcus had nowhere to go," I said to H. "I take it your boss told him to stay in town?"

H remained silent but glowered at Marcus.

"I'll make my own drink then," Marcus said to me. "Seeing as you're busy. I'll see you upstairs later." He went towards the kitchen and right up to Izzy who was still standing in the doorway with her phone in front of her, poised at Marcus, with her left eyebrow raised as high as it could possibly go.

Marcus stopped short, stared at her and pointed. "Do you know what? You could be Isabella Fallow's older sister." He cocked his head to one side. "Bit more make-up and you could pass as a poor-man's super model."

I gulped at the look on Izzy's face. I'd seen her look annoyed, fed up, bored but never angry. It was if she'd grown another three inches on her already tall height. Before my eyes, she morphed from serene swan to angry giant goose.

I stepped forward and yanked Marcus's arm, dragging him away. "Get upstairs and out of the way." I pushed him towards the hall.

"Hey, what's the issue?" He looked over his shoulder as we climbed the stairs. "What's got into that bird anyway? I gave her a compliment. I said she looked like a super-model. I thought she was going to slap me one."

Once in the bedroom I put my hands on my hips. "You idiot."

"What's wrong?"

"It *is* Isabella Fallows."

He took a sharp intake of breath. "How was I supposed to know you had a famous friend?"

"She wrote the article about me in the Daily News?"

"Who looks at the name of the journalist?"

After telling Marcus to drink from the bathroom tap if he was thirsty, I returned to the party.

"I'd better get off," H said in a monotone voice as he passed me the birthday cake. "I'm busy with the case."

I groaned as I watched him leave. Why did that man always make me feel bad? Now I felt as if I was harbouring a criminal. I had no idea who had killed Eddie Fly but I knew it wasn't Marcus, no matter how much I loathed him. H was wrong about him, and I had the feeling I would have to prove it if I wanted my life to get back on track. I took a deep breath and slapped on a smile, heading for the sideboard where

THE GHOST OF BRANDEN BAY | 89

the matches were kept. It was Jeff's party and I didn't want to spoil it for him by being grumpy. He had candles to blow out.

"Becky, thanks for inviting us," Andrew Farr said, he was standing next to the cupboard with the matches in. He had his arm around Katherine. They'd been childhood sweethearts but adult rivals who had recently joined together both romantically and in business. "Nice rugby tackle there on your cat. Do you play?"

I shook my head, smiling. "No, but I'm an only child to a rugby-mad father."

Andrew chuckled. "He taught you well. I'm so pleased you're joining in with the Victorian Town Theme Day. What will you be dressing up as? A fortune teller again?"

I laughed, when I'd dressed as a fortune teller at the fairground, I'd been swamped with fairgoers wanting to know their future. "Absolutely not. Lynn, Jeff and me, will be dressed as bakers. And I've hired a cart which Jeff is going to push around and sell cookies from."

"Are you still up for the planning meeting next week?"

"Whereabouts?"

"At the fairground," Katherine said. "The pier refurbishment isn't finished, but we're working on it so it's ready for the big day. The main damage was to the windows, they've been replaced and it's just decoration now. We've hired a chef to cook for us. It'll be a tasty meal."

"That sounds lovely. I'll be there." It would also be a chance to speak to the Levisons as I remembered Gina telling me she would be there. Something from the 1980's blasted from the speakers and Andrew dragged Katherine off to dance.

Annie danced over. "Was Andrew bending your ear about the Victorian Town Theme Day? It's all he's talking about."

"Yes, what will you be doing?" I asked. Annie was a manager tasked with integrating the pier with the funfair.

"General run-around, dealing with any crisis as it arises." She sipped her drink. "Hopefully it will go well and the sun will shine." She looked out at the rain lashing at the café windows.

"Good old British weather," I laughed. "They've invited me to the planning meeting next week."

"Great." She lowered her voice. "So why was your ex walking around in your dressing gown?"

"Marcus has been told not to leave town and had nowhere to go. He's sulking because I wouldn't let him join in with the party, so he made it ten times worse for me." I sighed. "I need to get these candles lit."

"Too late for that, hun. Jeff's unconscious on the kitchen floor. We'll have to save it."

I shook my head. "Look, I need a proper team meeting. Marcus isn't going anywhere and I'm being haunted nightly by Eddie."

"We're all here for you, Becky. We were great as a team on the last case."

"Lynn and me are planning another séance tomorrow night if you want to come." I felt myself slipping into the mystery, realising that I was well and truly taking on another case.

CHAPTER 9

"*B*ut it's easier if I stay here." Marcus pleaded with me over the kitchen table as Constance wailed from the snug. I'd locked her away so she couldn't attack our uninvited guest.

We ate Jeff's birthday cake for breakfast. The birthday boy had hailed it a successful hangover cure, before returning to bed wearing the new superhero dressing gown I'd bought him for his birthday, leaving me alone with Marcus. I'd stayed the night in Dannie's old room and would have had a great sleep if I hadn't spent most of the early hours plotting how to get rid of Marcus. At least I didn't see Eddie Fly, with Marcus sleeping in that room.

"I told you yesterday evening, that if you came downstairs, you would have to find somewhere else to stay. I can't have you under my roof. You've absolutely no respect for me, or my feelings."

"It won't be for long. If that copper friend of yours is as great as you make out." He sat back. "I must admit, I was jealous when I first met him. I thought you were together behind my back."

"It would hardly be behind your back, Marcus. Considering we're no longer a couple."

Marcus continued, as if I'd not spoken. "But seeing him with that fit bird at the restaurant. Wow, he's one lucky geezer."

I clenched my teeth together, pushing the repeated vision of Tara scooping dessert into H's mouth from my mind.

"Hey, babe. You're not jealous, are you? Just because I like the look of the copper's girlfriend?" He touched my hand.

I pulled it away. *Trust Marcus to assume it's all about him,* I thought.

"I hope he's as good as you say, because his questioning was a bit odd. He kept going off track."

"How?"

"He asked more questions about you and me than he did about Eddie Fly. Do you think he thinks you're my accomplice? Like Bonnie and Clyde?"

"What did he ask?"

"How long had we been together? Had we been engaged? Why did we split up?"

I'll be having words with him, I thought. "Sounds to me as if he was just being nosey." Or worse, double checking my story.

"I told him you'd become upset after your gran died and you didn't get promoted, so took time out." Marcus smiled at me. "Do you think we might get back together? I could set up a business here."

"No!" It came out as a shout. I stood up, clenching the sides of the table.

The back door opened, and Lynn appeared. "Is everything okay, lovey? I'm just setting the hut up for a service I've got this morning."

"Everything's fine," I said. "I'll be helping Marcus find somewhere else to stay, then I'm opening up."

"That's nice, lovey. Are we still on for tonight?"

"Yes. Marcus will be gone by then. See you later." I stood at the back door and watched her walk up the garden.

"But I'm skint," Marcus said from behind me.

I swung around. "Luckily, I'm not. My little backwater business, as you called it, is doing well. So, I'll pay. There's no way you'll be staying another night under my roof. Especially after last night's performance."

"I was hungry and thirsty." He gave me a doe-eyed expression. "I'm a hunted man. It's alright for you, having parties and living the simple life at the seaside."

Ignoring his comment, I didn't even flinch. I knew Marcus enjoyed the banter, and I didn't want him getting any sort of pleasure from arguing with me. "You can pay me back." I realised I was fast spending my reward money before it had even hit my bank account. But I'd rather borrow money out of the business and hit my credit card, than spend another night with Marcus.

Later, after he'd packed his holdall and was wearing freshly-laundered clothes, I handed over five hundred pounds, which I'd borrowed from the café takings. "That should last awhile. And here's the address of the hotel I booked." I felt an enormous sense of relief as I closed the door behind him. The small hotel was on the outskirts of town and, hopefully, I would not be bumping into Marcus around the bay.

LYNN ARRIVED at my house at nine for the séance. Dannie had travelled to Bristol to stay with her friend. She wasn't comfortable with the house having a resident ghost, especially not a naked one and I didn't blame her for being spooked.

"I hope it works this time, darling," Izzy said as she sat with Lynn and Annie. I gave them a nervous smile from the bathroom. Jeff stationed himself in the doorway, with his SLS camera on a tripod. Constance was next to me staring at the bath, as if waiting for Eddie to show.

"Five minutes to go," Jeff called from behind the camera.

"Hold hands, girls." Lynn performed a short protection prayer with Izzy and Annie. "Now everyone, think of Eddie Fly. In your mind, reach out to him. Invite him in."

Constance hissed.

I felt the buzzing in my fingers. "He's coming," I called as static filled my body and I gingerly turned around to face the bath. "The room has lit up," I said. "He's in the bath. Can you see him, Lynn?"

She opened her eyes and peered into the room. "No, I see no light at all. The rest of you, keep your eyes shut. Remain silent." She paused, shut her eyes and took in a deep breath. "Eddie, Eddie Fly. Can you hear me?"

"It's the same," I said. "He's singing in the bath, raising his leg and washing his foot."

Constance jumped onto the rim of the tub. Her coat fully bushed out.

I knew I needed to look closer at the scene to pick up any clues. I watched as Eddie scrubbed his foot with the loofa. "Hang on," I said. "He's got a massive scar-like patch on his leg. There's hair missing. It looks like burn tissue." I glanced over to see if I could see anything else before his gruesome death. "And there's a mobile phone on the side of the bath."

Lynn called out from behind me. "Edward Fly, we're here for you. We want to help. Please give us a sign that you can hear me. Anything."

Eddie's spirit looked towards me as he always did and he went through the same words I'd heard before.

"It's the same. Exactly the same," I said. My body buzzed like crazy. "Eddie, can you see me?"

"Get that knife away from me." Eddie put his hands up.

"Give us a sign," Lynn cried out.

"No. No. No," Eddie screamed.

I turned away and shut my eyes as Lynn carried on with her chanting and Constance continued with her wailing meow.

"He's gone," I said as darkness fell and Constance rubbed against my legs. I picked her up and found my heartbeat slow down as I stroked her.

"I'll get the lights," Jeff said and turned them on.

"That was quite something," Izzy said. "A real inside look at your gift, darling." She grabbed her notebook.

Annie hugged herself. "Must be awful for you, hun, having to relive that every night."

"I think it's time to move bedrooms, darling," Izzy said.

"What's your verdict?" Jeff said to Lynn as he switched on the light.

"He's a ghost," Lynn replied as Constance jumped onto her lap.

"I could have told you that," I said.

"His spirit is not here." She gave Constance a stroke. "We can't communicate with him. It's an imprint left. Not an actual spirit being. The energy is being picked up by the EMF meter, but if I'm right, Jeff, there was nothing to see on the camera?"

"Spot on," he said.

"I don't understand," Izzy said.

"It's like the difference between you being here, sitting opposite me, or me watching you at the movies. Like it's pre-recorded."

"Why's he in Becky's bathroom?" Annie asked.

She turned to me. "It's likely he attempted contact and failed." She sighed. "Although it doesn't mean we won't be able to contact him or help him move on to a better place. Ideally, we'll need a loved one present. None of us here really knew him."

I puffed out. "I feel like a failure."

"Lovey, not all spirits make contact. Clearly, in this case, it was an horrific end. He needs to reconcile."

"Still, I don't want his ghost in my bathroom."

"Why don't you ask his wife if she wants to make contact?" Annie asked.

"It seems a little disrespectful. He's only been gone a few days and apart from that, she made it quite clear, she's not interested in anything paranormal. I could call her though, to check how she's feeling and take it from there."

"Some people change their mind about the spirit world once they lose someone close," Lynn said.

"If what Marcus said was true, there was no love left between them," I replied. "But she's a suspect, so I'd like to interview her, anyway."

"Great idea," Izzy said.

"I'll call her first thing in the morning."

"So, are we still meeting?" Annie asked. "For a debrief?"

"Yes," I said. "Monday night."

. . .

It was Sunday lunchtime and I walked along the seafront. There were many people strolling along the prom. Residents, day-trippers, and holiday-makers were taking a trip to the bay, while the sun was actually shining. Dannie was covering for me. Jeff was up at the D.I.Y. store and Lynn was busy with a service at the spiritualist hut. It was the first time I'd left Dannie alone. *It's only for an hour,* I told myself as Constance poked her head out of my tote bag.

As I walked up the path to Carol's house, she opened the door. She'd clearly been waiting for me. She pulled me in by the hand, then put a finger up to her mouth. "Shhh."

"Why?" I whispered.

Constance meowed.

Carol smiled and scratched my cat's head. "Don't worry, I told H not to bring that awful woman with him."

I assumed she was referring to Tara. "She's his girl-friend," I whispered.

Carol huffed. "You're the only one for him. I can tell."

"I thought he'd be at work, what with a murderer on the loose."

"A man's got to eat."

"You're not still trying to match-make, are you?" I asked her.

"I see you as a daughter. I love you so much." She pulled me in for a hug.

Constance jumped out of my bag to the floor.

I chuckled. I'd only known Carol for a few months. "You can adopt me. Trust me, it's a lot easier than marriage. My parents won't mind, I'm sure."

She pulled me by the hand. "You look lovely," she said as she dragged me down the airy hallway and into the sitting room.

"Surprise!" Carol said.

Once inside the dining area in Carol's conservatory, I found Carol's husband, Paul. Their daughter Rachael, with her husband, seven-year-old twin boys and baby daughter. And, of course, H. He looked surprised to see me, but then his face broke into a small smile.

Constance sashayed up to him and rubbed herself against his legs, and he picked her up.

"Hi everyone." I gave a brief wave, then smoothed my hands down my skirt.

"I thought I'd get the whole family together," Carol said. "So, of course, I had to invite Becky." She stared in H's direction.

"I'm not really fam ..." I said.

"Nonsense, now sit down." Carol motioned towards the dining area. No surprises, she sat me next to H. Then took Constance to the kitchen to feed her.

"I thought you'd be at work," I said to H, as if I was making an excuse for invading his family get-together.

"Even the police get a lunch break," he said.

The meal was delicious, a traditional beef dinner with Yorkshire puddings, roast potatoes, and buttered veg. I ignored my troubles and noticed H smiling at me a lot. The boys chatted away about a party they'd attended at a play area while Paul told some really bad dad-jokes. I felt a warm glow, the type I got when spending time with my own family.

H's phone rang. "I'd better take this." He spoke to the caller in the lounge area, away from the table. I couldn't hear what he was saying, or lip read because he was turned away from me. He ran a hand through his hair and glanced back, but he wasn't smiling, his brow furrowed.

Rachael and her family went to play on the grass outside where Constance lay, spread out on a picnic rug in a pool of sunshine.

H approached me as a sickness settled into my stomach. "That was Brad," he said.

"Does he want me up for questioning?"

"Not yet." He hesitated.

"Come on, what is it? I won't tell anyone. I want this solved, thank you very much, so Marcus can leave town."

"So, you and he don't have a future?"

"I don't know what he's been telling you, or what it looks like. There's no future. We're done and have been for months."

"I don't blame the guy for trying. You're real girl-friend material."

I opened my mouth to say something, but Carol called out.

"Anyone ready for dessert? It's Baked Alaska."

"I can't, Ma, save me some." H replied.

"Henry. It'll only take five minutes to eat." Carol

tutted. "And you can't save Baked Alaska." She returned to the kitchen.

"So? Your call?" I asked him. "Can you solve this and get rid of Marcus?"

"They've found a weapon with blood on it. It's gone off to forensics, but they're pretty sure it's the knife used to kill Eddie Fly."

I put a hand up to my cheeks. "They might find fingerprints."

"That's the hope. It has a serrated edge. I'm only telling you this because we'll be putting an appeal out anyway, as the steak-knife comes from a hotel which isn't listed. The name of the hotel is branded on the blade."

I put a hand up to my throat. "It's not the Pilkington Hotel, is it?"

H's eyes widened. "How did you know? Did you see it in your psychic vision?"

I gulped and shook my head slowly. "It's the cutlery from Corelli's. Elena's uncle brought it with him when the hotel he worked for in London went bust."

H groaned. "I can see it now. You know what this means?"

I nodded my head. "Everyone in Corelli's that night is going to be a suspect and hauled in for questioning."

H looked grave. "Maybe. But this puts your ex-boyfriend, firmly in the frame. Staff found the knife at the Budget Inn. Keep the details of this to yourself until I've reported back to Brad. They may want to keep the details under wrap after all."

I nodded and watched him leave with Carol following him to the door with a paper bowl full of ice cream and meringue. I'd have to find the real killer soon or else Marcus was going straight to jail.

CHAPTER 10

*I*t was Monday, and the café was closed. The rain pelted down so I wasn't missing much trade. Jeff was at work on the early shift and Dannie was in her room, having been rushed off her feet the day before, helping with the café. When I'd returned from Carol's, it had taken a good half hour for me to sort out some disgruntled customers who had been waiting for their orders to arrive. Sighing, I realised I needed to focus more on my business and stop neglecting it.

I walked from the snug in my slippers with Constance in tow, then stopped as my landline rang. It was the call I'd been dreading, the one telling me I was required at the police station for questioning. My hand shook as I ended the call. The last thing I wanted was a grilling from D.C.I. Bad Cop Brad Harris. I didn't think the morning could get any worse until I walked into the café and found Marcus rapping on the glass doors.

Constance steamed over to the window, her coat bushing out.

I stared Marcus in the eyes and pointed to the sign on the door. "We're closed on Mondays," I shouted through the glass.

"Let me in," he shouted back.

I picked up a struggling Constance and unlocked the French doors.

"Good morning to you too, Becks." He ducked a swipe from Constance. "You need to train that cat of yours."

"She's very well behaved and popular with the customers. It's you she has a problem with." I scratched her head, trying to calm her down as she growled from my arms. "It's a long way from your hotel, isn't it? And I thought the booking included your meals."

"It was too far out. I found somewhere closer. Three doors up, the Harper."

"How did you afford that?" It was a small boutique hotel.

"I've gone for room only, no meals. I thought I could eat here."

"Well, you can't," I said as I took a struggling Constance and put her outside into the hall, then shut the door. "Especially not today when I'm closed. Don't you understand Marcus? I don't want to see you."

"But – "

"I've got to go out soon. Which is your fault, I might add, as the police want to question me about the murder."

"Sorry," he looked down at his feet.

"I haven't got time to make you anything, even if I wanted to." I didn't know if he knew that the Budget Inn staff had found the murder weapon and certainly didn't want to discuss it. "There's a greasy spoon café on the High Street.

I APPROACHED the desk at the police station. My palms were sweaty as I rubbed my hands together. H hadn't told Brad or anyone else about my vision of Eddie's death. I hadn't reported it officially and neither did I intend to.

"I'm here to see D.C.I. Harris," I said to the man at reception.

He made a call, then replaced the receiver. "Take a seat. He'll be out shortly."

I sat on a hard grey chair, which was screwed to the floor. The door squeaked, and I looked up. Brad filled the doorway. He had the face of a gangster upon a thick neck with a snake tattoo wrapped around it, as if it was strangling him. Before I found out he was a policeman, I thought he was a crook.

"Miss James," he growled.

I gulped and stood up. "Nice to see you again."

H appeared by my side.

"Just the man," said Brad. "I'm questioning Miss James."

"I know. I've come to assist."

"I've asked D.C. Wright to sit on this one. I'm afraid you're off the case."

H's chest rose and fell and his lips remained firmly together. He was clearly not impressed.

"Sorry," Brad said. "But you know the rules. I can't have you on a case where your girlfriend is a suspect."

"She's not my girlfriend. I've explained the position," H said.

"You're involved. You're being put on community."

H strode out of the reception without comment, clearly fuming. I could understand why, Branden Bay was his patch, Brad had waltzed in from Bristol, pushed him out of the way and there wasn't much H could do about it. After all, he was a newly-promoted sergeant and Brad not only had twenty years' experience but was also an award-winning detective chief inspector. He led me to an interview room.

Once inside, I faced Brad. "I'm not in a relationship with H, so he shouldn't be taken off the case because of me."

Brad's eyes looked amused. "I said his *girlfriend*, not *ex-girlfriend*." He chuckled. "Sit down, James."

My face flushed and I felt stupid. Tara had been at the restaurant too. She was obviously on his suspect list, not me. *I'm such an idiot,* I thought.

A woman police officer entered the room, who I guessed was D.C. Wright. She pointed behind her. "I've got the super on the phone."

Brad pushed himself up from the chair and

approached D.C. Wright. "Can you set the room up for an official interview?"

By the time D.C. Wright, who seemed really nice I might add and was definitely going to be playing the part of *good cop,* had set up the room and recording equipment, Brad reappeared and positioned himself directly opposite me.

"Do I need a lawyer?" I asked.

"You're not under arrest, and I'm confident that while you have the habit of turning up and poking your nose where it doesn't belong, you're not the killer. You're just a right royal pain in the –"

D.C. Wright interrupted Brad, with a short cough.

He took a deep breath. "You're here, because I want to build a profile of this boyfriend of yours, Marcus Day."

I gave a long sigh. "He's my ex-boyfriend. I met him a few years after I left university. I'd taken a receptionist job at a firm of accountants while I looked for acting work, and he was the head of the marketing department. We struck up a relationship. I guess he seemed older and knowledgeable, and I was flattered by the attention he gave me ..."

Brad sat back and crossed his arms over his broad chest. "I'm not interested in your sex life, James. I just want to build up a picture of the man." He leaned forward. "Is he desperate?"

I sat back and narrowed my eyes. Was he insinuating that he'd have to be desperate to date me? I took a deep breath and held it for five full seconds before exhaling slowly. The last thing I wanted to do, was wind up Bad Cop Brad. Even if he didn't have me down as a suspect, he could still make my life difficult. "He's a typical office boy, spends most of his time at work and his social time is spent schmoozing clients in wine bars. He plays golf. He's squeamish, he can't even kill a spider. He didn't do it. That's pretty much it."

D.C. Wright made notes, even though the interview was being recorded.

"And does he have a gambling habit?" Brad asked.

"Not that I know of."

"Any financial difficulties?"

I paused. Yes, he did. I rubbed the side of my neck. "He's recently lost his job."

"And how did he know the victim, Eddie Fly?"

"He was a potential client." I gestured towards D.C. Wright's notes. "I already told H, all of this."

"We require a statement. It was an off-the-record chat you had with D.S. Blake. I'm using correct procedures. And that was before we found the murder weapon." He paused, looking thoughtful. "You say it was a client meeting. But you also said Marcus Day had lost his job?"

"It's complicated."

"Try me."

I repeated what Marcus had told me.

"And you all ate at Corelli's wine bar?"

"Yes."

"And do you recognise this?" he pushed forward a photograph of a bloodied knife.

"Miss James is being shown the murder weapon," D.C. Wright said.

I nodded.

"Please reply, for the recording," she added.

"Yes. It's part of the cutlery at Corelli's." I pointed at the photograph. "But it can't be Marcus's."

"And why not?"

"He had soup," I said.

Brad laughed, a deep-throated chuckle, which I felt through my chest. The guy was humiliating me. I knew it was because of our history that I was the one to catch a killer and not him. *Stay calm.* I pursed my lips. "Soup is eaten with a spoon, not a knife."

"It's not Cluedo, Miss James." He shook his head. "He clearly had access to the cutlery. What did you eat?"

I paused. "Steak."

"Exactly," he said. "And I've been told you were sitting beside him?"

"Trust me, I know Marcus and he hasn't got it in him to kill."

"Of course not," Brad said in a slow voice. "And he's currently staying with you?"

"No, he's at the Harper Hotel."

Brad nodded at D.C. Wright and pointed to the tape machine.

After reading out the time for the record, she leaned to the right and switched it off

"Now, James," said Brad. "Keep out of my investigation, otherwise I'll be arresting you for wasting police time, no matter what excuse you have. Have I made myself clear?"

I nodded. "Can I go now?" I asked in a small voice.

ONCE HOME, the place was quiet, so I decided to go to the spiritualist hut to update Lynn. Opening the back door, I found Constance in her favourite spot underneath my apple tree, but she was standing rather than laying down, probably because it was spitting with rain. I picked her up and carried her to the back of the garden and through the gate. I walked up a few wooden steps to the entrance and pushed the door open.

The aroma of burning sage hit me as I walked in.

"Lovey, what a delightful surprise." Lynn placed a hand to her chest. "I wish I saw you in here more often. My congregation would love you to be here. They're always asking about you. It could really help with developing your gift if you helped channel the spirits for me."

I laughed. "You know that won't happen."

She sighed as Constance jumped down and approached her. "Your grandma didn't want to join the group either. Constance was very private with her gifts. But she solved a few murders herself."

"She did?"

Lynn nodded. "She never took credit for any of them. Always let Rushford take it."

"Who's he?"

"The police inspector of the day."

Hmmm, I thought. *Maybe I should let H and Brad take the credit.*

"No, dear," Lynn replied. "You should take the credit after the hard work you put in."

I frowned. Lynn really was psychic. I'd better watch what I thought.

Lynn laughed. "It doesn't take a mind reader to know what you're thinking, Becky. The look on your face tells it all. So, tell me what happened up at the police station?"

I filled her in on the interview.

"Are you going to leave it to the police, then?" Lynn asked when I was done.

"Of course not. Being warned off by Brad doesn't mean I'm going to stop trying to find Eddie's killer. In fact, it makes me want to find them even more."

"I guessed that would be the case." She grinned. "So, we're still on for the meeting tonight?"

"You bet we are." I had no intention of turning back.

CHAPTER 11

*I*t was the evening, and I'd made a cake for us to try, which had taken me the entire afternoon. Carolyn, a member of the Ladies Society, had given me the recipe having just returned from a trip to New Orleans. It was called a Mardi Gras cake, and comprised of two rows of rolled sweet dough, like a never-ending cinnamon swirl but filled with sugary dried fruit and nutmeg, covered in an icing glaze, which I'd decorated with coloured sugar in purple, green and gold. It received gasps of praise as my friends arrived for the meeting. I made a few pots of tea and we ate and chatted before we got down to business.

"Thanks for coming everyone," I said, once we'd eaten. They were all there. Izzy, Annie, Jeff and Lynn. Constance slept in the corner, snuggled up in her fluffy cat bed.

"I'm so excited that the investigation team is back

together," Izzy said as she gave my A-frame advertising board a wipe before directing Jeff to lift it on top of a café table to bring it to eye level.

"Is that entirely necessary?" I asked. I needed the board out front to display the daily specials.

"It's all about the visuals, sweetie. You should buy a proper white board for your business."

"It'll be tax deductible," Dannie added. "Having a murder board is an essential business expense."

Izzy stood beside the board like an assistant on a TV game show. "And thanks, Jeff, for the divine business cards." She held a card and gazed at it.

I shook my head. Jeff had handed out cards to Izzy, Lynn, Annie, and me. Dannie had made it quite clear, she didn't want a business card and was taking minutes and keeping records on a strictly freelance basis. She sat poised at the laptop.

I kicked off the meeting. "Eddie came from humble beginnings, won a lot of money on the horses and built a bookie empire. He was just about to open his next shop in Branden Bay High Street. According to H, he didn't always play by the rules. While taking a bath, he was killed by someone using a Corelli's steak knife. It was someone he planned to meet the following day. And he had a scar on his leg which looks like it was from a burn."

"So, who are our suspects?" Annie asked.

"We'll focus on whoever was at Corelli's that night, seeing as it was one of their knives that was used as the murder weapon. As we know, Marcus is the police's prime suspect. He was at the restaurant, he was at the murder site and they found the weapon on the grounds of the Budget Inn where he was staying."

There was a knock at the café glass door. I looked past Izzy. My shoulders drooped as soon as I saw it was Marcus peering through the window. "You're joking." I threw my hands up in the air.

Izzy looked at the door as if there was an intense, foul smell.

Constance raised her head from her fluffy bed and hissed.

I marched over and opened the café door. "We're shut and busy. You need to go back to your hotel."

"I've nowhere to go."

"You're registered three doors up." I began to close the door.

He put his foot on the threshold. "They ended my stay and gave me a refund. Seems someone tipped them off. No-one wants me here. They all think I'm a murderer

"Let him in," Annie called out. "You can question him."

I guessed she was right and stepped to one side. "Come in and sit down. We're going over the case. This entire investigation is for you," I said. "So don't make trouble." Okay, it was really for me so I could get rid of him and Eddie's ghost. "Now be helpful. Not rude."

Lynn had already scooped Constance in her arms.

Marcus approached Izzy. "I'm sorry Isabella. It was

dark at the party the other night ..." he trailed off as she ignored him.

"Sit down, Marcus," I said, pointing to a chair, as I took Constance from Lynn. "And you, Connie cat. You must not bite him, otherwise I'm locking you in the snug." I sat down, keeping a firm hand on my cat's back.

Lynn cut Marcus a chunk of Mardi Gras cake and pushed it on a plate across the table. He practically stuffed it into his mouth.

Izzy pulled a picture out of her bag and stuck it on the murder board. "As you said, sweetie, the police's prime suspect."

I sucked my lips in, to stop myself from laughing. It was a picture of Marcus in my purple crushed velvet dressing gown. An unflattering shot which showed his face contorted. I assumed he was mid-sentence, because his mouth was wonky and his eyes half open.

Izzy smiled sweetly at me. "I took it Friday night, darling. Well, it's a still from video footage. It took quite a few screenshots for me to get just the right pose." She turned and faced Marcus with a curt smile. "The police will no doubt have you back in the cells, since the murder weapon has been found at the Budget Inn."

"What?" Marcus looked at me as he spoke with his mouth full of cake.

"Izzy's right," I said. "The killer used a steak knife from Corelli's. It located you not only at the scene of the murder, but also at the site of the murder weapon."

He put his head in his hands. "This is bad, really bad. I'm done for."

"Are you sure he's innocent?" Lynn whispered to me.

"On the face of it, you look pretty guilty," Izzy said to Marcus – well and truly twisting the metaphorical knife.

He lifted his head. "Don't stick me on that board like I've done it. I've been framed. I'm the victim here," he whined.

"We need to treat you like all the suspects," I said. "So we can collect evidence to discount you. If the police had any solid evidence, trust me, you wouldn't be here. You'd be in a cell."

"Who else do you have on your list?" Marcus asked.

"Everyone in Corelli's starting with Fiona." I nodded at Izzy.

She placed a picture of Fiona on the A-frame. "I grabbed it from their social media page." It was a picture of Fiona opening a Fly's Flutters shop in Bristol.

"It's often the wife," Jeff added scratching his growing beard thoughtfully.

"There was a bit of tension between them," I said.

"A bit?" Marcus added. "I think demanding a divorce and asking her to clear her stuff out of their apartment is as tense as you get. And she's the one that shopped me to the police."

I nodded in agreement. "Blaming someone else is the oldest trick in the book. I've left a message with her to call me, as I want to interview her. I agree she has the motive. And Marcus, you said that Eddie told Fiona he was going to discuss the matter with her the following day, which makes her a significant suspect. I'll also do my best to convince her to join a séance."

Marcus sat up in his chair. "A séance? Don't tell me you really are into the occult? I thought the whole psychic thing was a marketing ploy."

I ignored him and continued. "Although Fiona made it quite clear when we had dinner that she doesn't believe."

"Who's next?" Annie asked.

"H," I said.

Dannie stopped typing. "You're joking, right?"

Izzy smiled at Marcus as she brought out the next photograph and stuck a picture of myself and H together, with him looking down and smiling at me as I grinned upwards. It looked as if we were staring longingly at each other. My cheeks flushed and burned as I stared at the picture. Izzy had been right. We did look like a proper couple in that snap.

"Absolutely gorgeous together," Izzy said.

"You should frame that one, Becky," added Lynn. "It's beautiful of the two of you."

Marcus frowned at the picture.

I pulled at my top. "He's not a suspect, but we still need to look at all the connections. He was with Tara." I paused. "His girlfriend."

Marcus exhaled and leaned back in his chair.

Izzy put a picture of Tara on the board. "I took this

one from her Insta." Tara was pouting at the screen with her eyes wide open and her chestnut hair was in its signature ponytail.

"She's definitely a suspect," I said, between gritted teeth.

Dannie raised her eyebrows. "Seriously?"

"Yes."

"Are you sure you're not a tad jealous?" Izzy drawled, giving a sideways glance at Marcus.

"Of course not." I shook my head a little too vigorously. "In fact, D.C.I. Harris has taken H off the case because his girlfriend is a suspect."

Annie frowned. "Oh dear, I bet H is mad about that."

"I want to know anything you can find out about her." I pushed my hair off my face. "While I was at the restaurant, she kept staring over at our table, giving a look full of hatred. I thought she was staring at me. But what if it was at Eddie?" I paused and lowered my voice. "What if she knew him?"

"And stabbed him to death," Jeff said, his eyes wide open.

"She's got a lot of muscle tone," Marcus said.

"She's a gym instructor," I said.

"I bet she could easily overpower a man." His eyes glazed over.

"Eddie wasn't that fit," I said.

"And a lot shorter than the leggy gym instructor," Marcus added.

"I'll check her social media for connections," Dannie said.

"Thanks. We can't discount anyone." I pointed to the board. "And what do we really know about Tara? She's only been in Branden Bay for a few weeks."

"I doubt very much that our H would date a criminal. He's an excellent judge of character," Lynn said. "Who else do we have?"

I checked my list. "Customer-wise, the only other table filled was with Councillor Nigel Levison and his wife, Gina."

Izzy stuck a picture of the couple dressed for a ball. "There's a bio of them on the Town Council's website. He's the next mayor. They take over the reins in a few months."

"I've met them socially," Lynn said. "They used to play bridge with me. They seem pleasant enough. I'm sure they were only at the bridge club for political reasons, but they were rather good at it, especially Gina. Do they have a connection with Eddie Fly other than eating at the same restaurant?"

"Yes. They knew him as he had meetings planned with them separately, the following day. Again, they are significant suspects."

Dannie typed away. "What did they want to discuss with Eddie?"

"Nigel wanted to talk about the betting shop and Gina said she wanted to discuss a private matter."

"They're doing a lot for the Victorian Themed Town Day," Annie said.

"Hmmm," I said. "It doesn't seem enough of a motive for murder. Disapproving of a betting shop in the High Street."

"They're very career-minded," Lynn said. "Power can go to people's heads."

"I'll quiz them at the meeting," I said.

"Who else was in the restaurant?" Dannie asked when she'd stopped typing.

"Elena, the owner."

Izzy put a picture of Elena up. "So beautiful."

"I'm pretty certain it's not her," I said.

"Is that it then?" Annie asked.

"No, there was a waitress who left after smashing a glass and a chef called Frank, who owed Eddie money and gave him a menacing stare. I'll go over to Corelli's tomorrow and see if I can interview them." I paused, looking at Jeff. "Would you like to come with me?"

"Yeah, great," he said beaming.

"Try to get some sneaky pics of them for the board," Izzy said, admiring her work on the A-frame, now full of faces with the suspect's names written underneath.

"I think that's enough for us to be getting along with," I said.

Annie smiled at me. "We've got this, Becky."

"I hope so," Marcus sighed. "Now, have you got anything for my dinner, Becky?"

Constance swiped at him. This time claw reached flesh and left a nasty scratch on the back of his hand.

CHAPTER 12

"*D*o not come out of this room, other than to use the bathroom," I said to Marcus. I'd moved him into the room which Dannie was originally sleeping in. "There's a jug of water and a sandwich platter with a selection of muffins on the table. Plus my iPad to stream films on."

"It's like I'm under house arrest," he huffed. "Mind you, with that monster cat on the loose, I don't want to come out of the room." He held up his hand, which had a plaster on it.

"Don't be such a baby, it's only a scratch. Now promise me you'll stay in here."

"But, Becks. I get claustrophobic."

"I don't care. If it wasn't for you chasing Eddie as a client – who was a hopeless case, I might add – we wouldn't be in this mess. And if you don't let me get on with it, you'll be in a much smaller room than this, and goodness who knows who you'll have to share with. But I'm guessing, they'll be a murderer."

"Thanks for making me feel much better." Marcus visibly shuddered. "What if I want to stretch my legs?"

"You'll have to wait for me to get back. It's not fair on Dannie to have you wandering around the house making a nuisance of yourself. And there's no way Lynn wants you getting under her feet in the café."

"I could be the maître d'."

"Oh no. You're considered a person of interest in a murder investigation. As with the other establishments around town, I'm not keen on showing you off. Either, you stay in this room when I'm out of the house or find somewhere else to live." Oh, how the tables had turned. In London, it was always him dishing out the orders.

TEN MINUTES LATER, Jeff and I entered Corelli's. I looked over at the table I'd sat at with Marcus and the Flys, then shook away the memory.

Elena nodded at me. "You have come to question me, Becky?"

Undertaking my investigation discreetly was impossible since I was now well-known around town as an investigator. I nodded. "If you don't mind?"

"It's quiet today. Are you eating?"

"Yes," Jeff said, before I could say we only wanted coffee.

Elena showed us to a table for three. "I will join

you. This death has brought back memories of Robert." Elena's lover had been murdered a couple of months previously. "If I can help in any way. I will do. I will bring cannelloni, we have extra, so there will be no charge."

After the three of us had eaten the lunch-time special filled with ricotta cheese, Elena poured us water from a bottle. It hadn't seemed right to talk about death while we were eating, so we'd discussed the upcoming Victorian Town Theme Day. Elena was looking forward to it. I had to hand it to Andrew Farr. He could be pushy, but he was great for the local economy.

"So, Elena," I said, getting my phone out and bringing up my note-taking app. "Obviously, I know the guests that were here. Were any of them acting suspiciously, do you think?"

"The policeman and gym instructor appeared to be having a lovely evening together," she said.

I didn't really want to hear about that. "What about Councillor Levison and his wife, Gina?"

"There was tension there. Whenever I went over to the table, they stopped talking. I don't think they cared very much for Eddie Fly. I heard his name mentioned."

"What about the waitress?" Jeff asked.

"Molly? She's been here for a couple of weeks only." She took a sip of water.

"She went home. Why was that?" I asked.

Elena shifted in her seat. "I, er ..."

"You didn't sack her then, after what Fiona Fly said?"

"No, of course not. But she's not been in since, because of personal issues."

"Where does she live?" Jeff asked.

"Bristol."

"Did she know Eddie Fly?" I asked.

Elena took another sip of her water. "I am not one to spread gossip."

"Did she dislike Eddie?" I asked in a gentle voice, trying to tease it out of her.

Elena puffed out. "Okay, I see you will not leave it. I understand." She took a deep breath. "Molly became upset, very upset, after she had been to your table. She said Eddie Fly did not have a heart. She collapsed into sobs. I told her to go home. We were not busy, after all."

"So, what exactly was she crying about?" I asked.

"I have no idea. I did not ask. But I sense." She put a hand to her chest. "They had a history."

"What's Molly's full name?" Jeff asked.

"Molly O'Brien."

"And what age is she?" he added.

"Thirty-five."

"Have the police asked about her?" I said.

"They asked me to identify the murder weapon and asked for the names and contact details of everyone at the restaurant that night. They did not ask for my observations."

"Probably because they think they have already

identified Marcus as the culprit. However, that's sloppy of the police." I noted this on my phone. "Do you think Molly would speak to me?"

"She said she would be back for the Victorian Town Theme Day."

"I'm guessing the only other person in the restaurant that night, was the chef?"

"Yes, Frank DuPont."

"Is he here now?" I asked, looking in the direction of the kitchen.

"He only covers for the main chef on a Wednesday."

"Where does he normally work?"

"He's a private chef. I understand he works in many places. Both here and in Bristol."

"Did he know Eddie?" Jeff asked.

"When Molly was upset, he comforted her and said a few harsh words. He said Eddie Fly had a lot to answer for. And then said something in French ..." she hesitated.

"Go on?"

"My French is limited but the tone of his voice told me that Eddie Fly was not his favourite person."

"Interesting. And did you tell the police this?" I asked.

"No. I am sure they will discover Frank's views when they question him."

"Can you give him my card and ask him to call me?" I handed her the purple card Jeff had designed.

"Would you like dessert?" she asked.

It would have been rude not to, and I ordered a bowl of chocolate and vanilla gelato.

As Jeff and I walked home, with a pizza I'd bought to take away, I turned to him. "We've got a lot to go on. Firstly, Molly would appear to have had some sort of romance with Eddie."

"Do you think his wife knew?"

"If she did, it would explain why she was so nasty about Molly. Eddie was quiet during the whole episode." I tried to picture what happened. "And they started arguing after Fiona said that she didn't measure up."

"Do you think he was having an affair with her?"

"That's something I intend to find out." My phone rang. "Great timing." I picked it up "Fiona, how are you?"

"It's dreadful, Becky. I'm sorry I did not call you back sooner. The police have been over today for more questioning. They ask such personal things."

"Like what?" I stopped in a shop doorway and Jeff put his ear up to the other side of the phone so he could hear.

"About my relationship with Ed. It's not on when I'm experiencing such loss and the shock of seeing him like that." Her voice cracked. "Have they questioned you as well?"

"Yes, they have. Would you like me to come over?" I asked.

"Oh, would you? That would be amazing. I have a

theory which the police have dismissed. I'm sure you'll check it out, even if they won't."

I arranged to meet her in an hour, hoping Lynn didn't mind covering the café for the rest of the day. I realised I should put her wages up.

When we reached home, I went upstairs, to find Marcus sprawled on the bed, eating popcorn and watching a horror film on my iPad.

He looked up. "How did you get on? Any leads?"

I nodded. "It was very interesting. And I'm off to meet Fiona."

"Can I come?"

I shook my head. "No. You stay here out of trouble. I brought you a takeout pizza from Corelli's." I handed him the box.

An hour later, Jeff and I reached Bristol, driving alongside the harbour with the SS Great Britain ship on our right. Constance sat on the dash. I'd had to bring her with me because I could not expect Lynn to keep an eye on her any longer.

I looked at the map app on my phone. "It's one of those flash apartments with balconies overlooking the harbourside."

"I can't park in the multi-storey; the van is too tall. I'll drop you and then park at College Green."

"Will you be alright waiting in the van with Constance?"

My cat hissed.

"Look, Connie cat, I can't take you into some swanky flat."

Jeff dropped me outside the apartment block. I walked up to the entrance and buzzed Fiona's apartment.

Fiona answered the intercom. "You're early." She paused. "Come on up, it's the penthouse."

Once inside, the lift opened, and a man came out with his head down, wearing a tweed flat cap.

"Good morning," I said.

He didn't even look up or acknowledge me. I tutted as the lift doors closed. It was obviously the sort of neighbourhood where you did not pass the time of day with anyone. I pressed the button for the penthouse.

As I came out of the lift, I heard electric power tools.

Fiona waved me into her beautiful apartment. There were workmen fitting kitchen cabinets. "I've always wanted an industrial style kitchen," she said.

She was having aluminium worktops installed and two large ovens side by side. Clearly, she liked to cook. Her set-up was looking somewhat more professional than mine and I was a caterer. I stared at Fiona, who had her hair tied up and wore glasses.

"Let's have coffee. I'll order it in. There's a shop downstairs, they'll send it up for me." She phoned down an order for our coffees and then led me to a huge lounge, which had views of the small city harbour. The whole area had been turned into a luxury living space, a far cry from the days of trade.

She sat beside me on the grey fabric sofa. "What a nasty business. I still can't believe it."

"I know. If you don't mind, I want to get a picture of everyone at Corelli's that night." I pulled out my phone to take notes. "I take it Eddie wasn't popular with Councillor Levison?"

Fiona laughed. "And the rest of the Council."

"Why did Mrs Levison want to meet Eddie?"

"You'll have to ask Gina yourself."

"How well did Eddie know her?"

"They went back a long way. He knew her way before I met him and before she met Nigel. I think they met at church." She touched the back of her head. "I've never been that keen on her myself. He saw a lot less of her after we became an item. I hadn't seen her for over a year."

"So, there was nothing ever romantic between them?"

Fiona gave a short, sarcastic laugh. "You have seen her?"

I pictured Gina in my head. I guess she was nowhere near as glamorous as Fiona. "And the waitress? Had you seen her before?"

"The Italian?" Fiona said in an airy voice.

"No. The one who dropped the glass."

She frowned and moved her hair from her forehead. "I recognised her, vaguely, maybe. You see so many people these days. It's often difficult to place them."

"So, you and Eddie were getting a divorce?"

Fiona laughed. "Not at all, where on earth did you get that idea?"

"Marcus."

"Eddie threatened to divorce me on a weekly basis. It was just the fire in our relationship." She sighed. "The making up was always so sweet." She removed her glasses and dabbed her eyes. "He loved me. He'd never have left me."

"Right," I said slowly. "And what about the chef, Frank DuPont?"

"He worked for us briefly." She scratched her forehead. "I recognised that girl in there, though," she added.

I frowned. "Who?"

"The one with the totally gorgeous guy. Mister tall, dark and handsome. Oh ... My ... Goodness. If only I was ten years younger."

I raised my eyebrows. She was of course talking about H. "He was with Tara? You know her?"

"I recognise her from somewhere. And the name, now you come to mention it."

"She's a gym instructor. She works at Millar's."

Fiona shook her head. "No, I've not been to Millar's gym. It'll come to me. I'll let you know."

"She lives in Bristol," I said, not wanting to drop the matter.

"Well, that's probably it. She must be a neighbour or something."

"Who do you think hated Eddie enough to kill him?" I asked.

Fiona sighed. "Unfortunately, plenty of people. But there's one in particular that I think could be involved and I wanted to tell you about him, because I take it you'll pursuing this?"

"Absolutely."

She huffed. "I told my husband so many times, 'Eddie, you can't tread on people like that.' But he never listened." She sighed. "He always said to get on in life, you needed to be ruthless, and he'd come so far." She turned to me. "You know, he was homeless as a child for a time. He literally came from nothing." She took a deep breath, which caught in her throat. "I used to dig at him for being so ... well ... basic. But you have to admire that about him."

"Where does his family live?"

She shrugged. "He told me his mother was dead and he never knew his father. He refused to discuss anything before his time with the Wrights."

"Who are the Wrights?"

"A vicar and his wife, they took him in. I don't know where exactly, I never met them and have no idea what happened to them."

I made a note of that on my phone. "Who in particular do you think killed him?"

She sat back in her seat. "I'm convinced it was Connor Davies." She paused. "The man himself has already been in touch, asking about buying the betting shops. But the police dismissed that theory."

"Who's Connor Davies?"

"Someone a cut above Eddie." She stood up and

hugged herself. "He doesn't have betting shops but has a large casino here in Bristol. Eddie wanted to branch out to casinos himself. There's silly money in that business. And a lot more prestige. Eddie wanted to up his game, even though he had already done brilliantly. We're quite rich now." She paused, then lowered her voice. "Or should I say, I am?"

There was a buzz at the intercom, and Fiona went to the front door to collect the coffees she had ordered. I looked around the room to find there was not one photograph of Eddie.

She returned and handed me a coffee in a takeout cup.

"Thank you. So, this Connor Davies. Do you think he would kill off his competition?"

"He'd get one of his goons to do the dirty work. He's a professional and will have a rock-solid alibi, no doubt. Eddie wouldn't be the first person winding up dead who got on the wrong side of him."

"Did Eddie have dealings with him before he died?" I asked, then took a sip of my latte.

"Eddie was jealous of Connor. He was forever following his business deals. We used to visit the casino and he'd watch the guy all night like a hawk. Connor is easy to spot, he wears a white dinner jacket and blue bow tie. It's his signature look. Back home, Eddie would look up the public record of Connor's accounts online and pour over them, trying to calculate what it would cost to run such an establishment. Eddie wanted to be the top dog. He was out to prove he could be whatever he wanted to be. And ..."

"What?"

She shuddered. "Connor threatened Eddie recently. He said he'd kill him before allowing him to open a casino within one hundred miles of Bristol."

Deep down, like the police, I thought it was someone who was at Corelli's because of the weapon they'd used. But I wanted to take a closer look at this new suspect.

"Now, was there anything else? I really must get back to the kitchen and oversee the renovation."

I stood up. "We could try to contact Eddie's spirit to find out who killed him?" I threw it in there. "I have a friend that could help. It's only going to work if we have a loved one present."

She blinked. "Absolutely not. It's not for me. I don't believe in any of that rhubarb." She dabbed her eyes with a tissue.

I texted Jeff once I was outside the apartment. Fiona had told me she was coming over to Branden Bay for the Victorian Town Theme Day and would pop into the café and said she would let me know if she remembered where she knew Tara from. As I made my way to the main road, I felt a fire of excitement lighting inside. The thrill of being on a fresh case was hard to ignore. I brushed it aside as I saw the van approach.

"Did she agree to the séance?" Jeff asked as I climbed in.

Constance jumped onto my lap as I sat down.

"No, she's definitely against it. But I have a whole bunch of leads to be going on with." I clicked my seat-belt in.

"Like what?"

"Fiona thinks Eddie was killed for stepping on the toes of a gangster casino owner called Connor Davies. Eddie knew Gina Levison before she met Nigel. Eddie was homeless as a child and was taken in by a vicar and Fiona thinks she recognises Tara."

"Where from?"

"She can't remember, but said she'll let me know when it comes to mind."

"What about the waitress and chef?"

"Hmm, she recognises the waitress but can't place her and when I questioned her about Frank DuPont, she appeared stiff, giving me a brief reply. I got the impression she was hiding something. I don't trust Fiona at all."

"So, do you think we have a new suspect with this Connor guy?"

"He gave Eddie a death threat. I certainly intend to visit the casino to check him out."

CHAPTER 13

The sun was low in the sky as I walked arm in arm with Annie along the prom to the Victorian Town Theme Day planning meeting. We heard the works going on at the pier as we passed. Annie told me that they were working around the clock to get it ready for the event. Constance poked her head out of my tote bag, I didn't want to leave her back at the house with Marcus there, and knew Katherine and Andrew were fine with her.

Andrew met us at the entrance of the fair's administration buildings. "Come in," he said. "Hang your coats up. We're in the staff meeting room and have set the boardroom table for dinner."

Constance poked her head out of my bag.

"Ah, your trusted side-kick." He scratched the top of her head and she gave a loud purr.

I laughed. "I've brought her food with me. She'll be good, I'm sure."

As I put my coat on the hanger, I noticed a tweed flat cap. *Clearly a fashion item these days,* I thought. I was seeing them everywhere.

As we entered the room, I noticed Nigel Levison sitting at the end of the table.

"Hi." I stuck my hand out to shake his. "We haven't spoken before."

Constance jumped to the floor.

"Ah yes. You ate with Eddie Fly before he passed away."

I sat next to him, wondering where his wife, Gina was. "It's very sad."

Constance jumped onto my lap, and I stroked her.

Levison nodded. "I gather this Marcus fellow, who you dined with that evening, is the prime suspect."

"He's innocent," I said.

Levison tapped my hand. "It's difficult when those we love act out of character."

I pulled my hand away. "No really. Marcus didn't do it."

Levison continued as if I'd said nothing. "I've had contact from the police myself, this afternoon. To give my evidence and observations. I saw Marcus leaving the restaurant with Eddie and Fiona."

Constance hissed. I presumed at the sound of Marcus's name. It appeared that everyone thought he'd done it, except me.

"I've known Marcus personally for years. I don't think it's him. And the police have nothing solid on him, otherwise he'd be in the cells. They don't want people to realise they're clueless about who really did it." I stroked Constance's head.

"Hopefully, they'll find the evidence they need soon, to put the man who did it behind bars."

"Or woman," I said. "How's your wife?"

Levison frowned at me.

I thought I'd give him some of his own medicine.

"She's on a spa break," he said leaning back in his chair.

I thought it odd, seeing as she specifically said she would be at the meeting. "I guess the police will question her, especially as she was close to Eddie Fly."

"My wife was not close to Fly."

"I hear she knew him a long time before she met you."

Levison's eye twitched. "They no longer had a connection."

"In Corelli's, she arranged to meet Eddie the following day. I was sitting there listening."

Levison ran a finger around the rim of his glass, which made a noise that Constance clearly didn't like as she swiped at his hand. He pushed his glass out of her reach. "Maybe you should leave your cat at home." He huffed. "As you observed, Gina indeed approached Eddie. I told her not to, but she's raising funds for a charity event." He turned to me. "My wife does good works. Did you know him well?" he asked me.

"No," I replied. "It's the first time I met him. Were you ever friends with Eddie?"

Annie sat beside me and Constance thankfully jumped onto her lap.

Levison laughed. "I wouldn't call us friends. As I said to the police, we socialised briefly when I began courting Gina and lost touch when Gina and I moved from Bristol to make our home in Branden Bay. I can assure you, that we move in totally different circles. Eddie made contact recently, wanting support for the betting shop in the High Street, and thought, incorrectly, that he could buy my support."

"So he offered you money?"

Levison sat back. "I told the police everything. One must be careful when entering local politics." He drank from his wine glass. "I understand, Miss James, that you consider yourself an amateur sleuth."

"Erm, well ..." I guessed it came across as if I was interrogating him.

"So, how does that rest with the police?"

I gave a short laugh. "I have personal reasons for wanting the actual killer to be found, and it's in my nature to pursue that."

"You should be careful. My opinion is that Eddie Fly was one rough stone that could never be polished into a diamond." He looked me in the eye. "Talking of diamonds, I hear you came into quite a hefty reward?"

Annie butted in. "She's sharing it with all of us."

"Very admirable." He raised his glass at me.

Izzy glided into the room and approached us, as the staff distributed the starters.

"Just in time," Annie said as Izzy sat beside her.

When I looked back to my right, Nigel Levison had moved seats and was chatting to Katherine. I was happy that I'd managed to speak to him, I certainly got the vibe that he disliked Eddie and hated him being anywhere near his wife. I wanted to speak to Gina Levison as soon as I could. I felt there was a lot more to her history with Eddie than Cllr Levison was letting on.

The starter was simple, a duck terrine with French toast. It had an amazing orange infused chutney with it. After we'd eaten the first course, Andrew addressed us all.

"I'm happy to announce that after Nigel pulled a few strings, both the High Street and Beach Road will be free of general traffic for the event."

Everyone clapped, and Nigel Levison raised his glass.

Andrew continued. "I've a classic car firm who will drive an old Victorian car and we have a collection of horse and carts. They'll charge for rides, so we don't have to pay for their use. I've printed a list of all the businesses in town, with those who are in with us, and those who have yet to confirm."

"Also," Katherine said. "I'm pleased to report that Somerset Steam Railway will travel to and from Bristol to bring people in. And the old steam ferry is coming across from Wales, assuming the pier refurbishment finishes on time. We're arranging a set of prizes for the best dressed in town to encourage visitors to wear Victorian attire."

Izzy smiled at everyone. "And I can add that the Gazette will be there with myself covering the event in its entirety. All in all, it's going to be a very exciting day indeed for Branden Bay."

"The event is going to be amazing," I called down the table to Andrew.

"I'll tell the chef we're ready for the main," Katherine said.

The door swung open, and H appeared.

"Ah, the police representative," Andrew said. "I wasn't expecting a detective." He added, running a hand through his wayward blond hair.

H nodded a hello at Andrew before taking the seat next to me, where Levison had been sitting. "I've you to blame for this. Since they've taken me off the current case, I'm in limbo."

"This is good, isn't it?" I said. "You get a free meal."

"I didn't join the force to take part in fancy dinners."

I swallowed. "Brad took you off because of Tara, not me."

"Trust me. It was because of you," he said as he was served the main course.

"Once this case is wrapped up, things should be fine," I said as a waft of Beef Bourguignon reached me.

"There'll be another one. And no doubt you'll be all over that as well."

"It's not my fault I see dead people."

He sighed. "I never said it was your fault that they associated me with you."

Hmm, associated? I thought. You wouldn't use that to describe someone you were romantically attracted to. Sounds more like a dodgy relative you wish you never had. "Brad said Tara is a suspect. Why's that?"

"Everyone in Corelli's that night is a suspect. He even had me prepare a statement."

"Did Tara have steak?"

"Becky, drop it. Tara didn't kill Eddie Fly."

"Someone killed him, and it wasn't Marcus."

"Fly wasn't popular."

"So I've heard." I didn't mention Connor Davies.

"Look, if we have to pull you out of anything, Brad will charge you with wasting police time."

We ate our meals in silence as Izzy and Annie chatted to each. other.

Andrew stood up once we had finished out main course. "We need to discuss timings. The streets will be closed first thing to allow the stalls to set up. And the first train rolls in at half past nine. Nigel will officially open the event at ten. We've local amateur groups providing brief shows on a temporary stage, which will be set up on the beach."

"That's great," I said. "This whole day will be amazing. I just can't wait." Then smiled as the dessert of crème caramel was delivered to the table.

· · ·

ONCE HOME, I changed and got ready for bed, then went downstairs to the snug, closing the door behind me. I was due a video call from my parents. Constance jumped onto my lap, and I sat back just as the call came through.

"Mum, Dad." I waved at them and smiled as I looked at their tanned faces on the screen. "How's it going in Australia?"

"It's amazing," Mum said.

"It'd be better if you were here," Dad said. "We were just saying how you should come over and spend time with us. Why not get a flight out in a week or so?"

"I can't really leave the café," I said, not wanting to tell them the real reason would be that I had Marcus staying and he'd been accused of murder. They knew nothing of what had been going on since I'd moved to Branden Bay. I didn't want them to worry about spirits and a dead body. I hoped that now they were back to civilisation and out of the jungle, they wouldn't be catching up on any UK news.

Constance poked her head in front of the smartphone camera.

"Aw, you still have the cute cat," Mum said.

Dad frowned at the screen then rubbed his eyes as Constance jumped to the ground.

"You alright, Dad?" I asked.

"Where did you say that cat came from again?"

"She just turned up at the back door, remember? I named her Constance after Grandma."

Dad mopped his brow and Mum updated me on

their travels. I loved listening to their stories and missed my parents so much I ached inside. It was less than four months until they returned. After speaking to them, I laid back on the sofa, pulled the blanket over me and fell asleep. I couldn't face another night of Eddie Fly.

AFTER A BUSY AND SUNNY DAY, I closed the café. I'd called Elena at Corelli's, earlier in the day, and asked if I could go in and question the chef. She'd explained that he'd doubled his rates and she could no longer afford him. "It seems he's in much demand," she'd said. "But you saw how many covers I took last Wednesday. It's not viable. I'll probably have to shut midweek." She'd sounded harassed and said she was phoning around to find a replacement before making a final decision. I'd have to wait until the Victorian Town Theme Day to interview Molly. And I needed to locate Frank, the chef.

I'd made a simple quiche and salad for Dannie, Jeff and Marcus for their tea. They ate their meal in the café. Marcus was quiet. I felt sorry for him and then reminded myself how he'd treated me.

"You look nice," he said as I placed Constance in my tote bag.

"I'm off to Izzy's for a meal," I replied.

"You're always out."

"Is H going to be there?" Dannie asked.

"Yes. He's picking me up."

Marcus huffed.

"I bet the food at Izzy's is going to be proper lush with her being a food critic," Dannie said. "What's she cooking?"

"I don't know." I hoped it was something I liked and didn't involve snails, caviar or truffle.

I heard the hoot of H's car horn. "I'll see you tomorrow. Don't wait up."

Outside, I eased myself into the passenger seat and Constance purred at H, I'd brought her cat bed as I didn't want her to mess up Izzy's furnishings.

"Hi there," I said to H. "I'm looking forward to this meal." Every month, the group of friends had dinner at each other's houses and since I'd moved to Branden Bay, they'd included me. Annie had made us a lovely home-cooked stew, I'd dished up a roast, and we'd been to H's for a BBQ. "I'm expecting restaurant quality."

H laughed. "It'll certainly be that." He slowed the car as we reached Annie's apartment, where she waited for us on the pavement.

"Hi guys," she said as she got in the back. "I'm so looking forward to this I've been rushed off my feet organising the Victorian Town Theme Day."

I turned to H. "Are you dressing up for it? You looked great as the Phantom of the Opera at the Summer Masked Ball." A vision of H in costume flashed into my mind, and I blushed.

"I won't be there. I'm being sent on a two-week secondment to cover the Devon force," he said as he took Castle Road, leading up to the poshest street in town where Izzy's apartment was situated.

"That's miles away." There was a burning sensation in my stomach. I widened my eyes. I wondered whether he'd take Tara with him and we sat in silence for a while.

"So, what's the latest on the case?" Annie asked.

"I know as much as you do," H said as he killed the engine outside of Izzy's place. "Let's leave the subject in the car."

"I wonder what sort of food we'll be getting?" I said as we entered the lift.

"Italian," Annie said.

"How do you know that?"

"She always does Italian," H said.

As the lift opened, I sniffed the air. "I can't smell it cooking?"

H coughed, and Annie giggled.

"What's funny about that?" I asked.

Annie put her arm in mine. "Come on, it's just us being silly."

Izzy flung open her door. "Darlings, come on in. I have Bollinger."

"I can't drink," H said. "I'm driving."

"Never mind, more for us." Izzy waved us in.

I walked in and saw that Izzy had set the table, and in the centre was a salad and garlic pizza.

"Help yourselves to a glass I've already poured. I'll take the lasagne out of the oven.

I set Constance's bed down away from the table

and plonked her in it. "Stay." I'd given her a double serving of salmon before we came out and she proceeded to groom herself so I knew she was just about to settle down for a nap. I felt a sigh of relief as I walked over to the table, sat down and took a gulp of my glass of fizz. "You've dressed the table amazingly, Izzy."

"I do have an artistic touch, don't I?" she said, as she carried over the lasagne.

"Wow, that smells amazing," I said, as Izzy placed the dish on the table. "And you've kept the place so clean." I admired the shiny marble worktop. "I make a right mess when I cook lasagne. Especially that pesky white sauce you have to stir so quickly. I get splatters of it everywhere, then add to it, with the bubbling tomato sauce."

"Preparing well in advance is my strategy." She smiled at me. "Then I can enjoy more time with my guests. Tuck in sweeties, don't let it go cold."

I had to admit the meal was divine and really was restaurant quality.

I sighed as I munched on the lasagne, swallowed, and took a sip of champagne. "This is as good as Corelli's," I said.

Annie seemed to stifle a sneeze.

H rubbed her back and gave a short cough.

"Are you okay?" Izzy asked them with a frown.

Annie blinked away a tear. "I think I breathed in a bit of black pepper or something."

I didn't know what was wrong with H and Annie. I

sensed they had some sort of in-joke that myself and Izzy were being kept out of.

I turned to Izzy. "Have you got anything on Councillor Levison? We saw him last night, and he didn't exactly seem upset that Eddie was dead."

H finished his mouthful of food and put his fork down. "I told you, let's keep the case out of it."

"Darling, it's in her blood. Becky James can't just sit by when there's been an injustice."

"It sounds like the start of one of your articles," he said. "More like you want to sell another story to a national paper. Let's talk about something else." H turned to me. "What are you doing with your life, Becky, that doesn't involve sticking your nose into police business?"

"I'm busy with the café, of course; there's the Victorian Town Theme Day, and I'm selling some of Grandma's antiques at auction."

Izzy placed her hand on my arm. "Darling, I love a good auction. Can I tag along?"

"That'd be great." I smiled.

"Don't you think it'll be emotional to watch?" Annie asked.

I nodded. "The auctioneer said the only sellers that turn up are the one's desperate for a sale. But I want to be there, to see where Grandma's things will be going."

I finished my meal and noticed there was a dessert spoon. "We have something sweet to follow?"

"Yes, darling. I made it this morning. A tiramisu."

"Izzy, you're a dream," I said. I wasn't let down.

Izzy's tiramisu also tasted restaurant quality. In fact, it was so nice that I missed my mouth as I scooped the cream and coffee loveliness into my mouth. I looked down at the posh silver embroidered napkin on my lap. I didn't want to spoil it, it might stain.

Annie laughed. "Here." She pulled a tissue from her bag. "Wipe it up with this."

"Do you want me to make coffee?" H asked Izzy.

"Yes, please." She nodded. "But we'll drink it at the table."

Izzy had white soft furnishings wherever you looked. I'd never had a coffee or tea there before.

"I'll get rid of this tissue." I stood up and followed H through to a small utility room. It was again posh with marble worktops and integrated cupboards. "Do you know where the bin is?" I asked him.

He pulled out a large drawer with separate bins inside. As I placed the tissue in the trash, I noticed the array of folded plain brown takeaway boxes in the recycling section. I looked up at H.

He grinned and nodded. "Yep, it doesn't taste like Corelli's without good reason," he whispered.

"Hope you two are behaving yourselves in there," Izzy called out in a suggestive tone.

I laughed as I helped H make coffee.

"Izzy can't even toast a slice of bread. Let alone cook a meal," he said.

"But she's always digging you about your cooking?"

"A smokescreen. But we play along with it. It's not worth upsetting her."

The rest of the evening went well, and we played a couple of card games. I noticed how good Annie was at poker. She always won when we played. I'd decided who I needed to ask to join me at the casino to help me check out Connor Davies.

CHAPTER 14

I made an excuse about wanting Annie's opinion on the Victorian baker outfits I'd bought for the Victorian Town Theme Day, so after we left Izzy's place, H dropped her at mine.

Once inside, I turned to her. "Do you want to come to the casino with me tomorrow night?"

"Are you taking up gambling?" Annie asked. "Have I led you astray?"

I laughed. "No." I took her by the hand as we followed a meowing Constance to the kitchen. "When I went to Fiona's yesterday, she said that Eddie rubbed a casino owner up the wrong way. She reckons he paid one of his goons to knock Eddie off." In the kitchen, I brought his picture up on my phone from the Casino website. "Here," I said, passing the phone to Annie. "His name is Connor Davies."

"He looks like a typical bad guy to me." Annie put the phone close to her face.

In the picture Connor Davies wore the white dinner jacket and electric blue bow tie, Fiona had told me about. "Exactly," I said. "I want to observe him and see if I can sense any bad vibes."

Constance meowed as I filled her bowl with water.

"That sounds dangerous, hun."

"I won't interrogate him or even speak to the guy. I thought we could float around the casino as an observation exercise."

Annie frowned and remained silent.

"I'm going, whether you're coming with me or not," I said as I watched Constance go through the cat flap to the garden.

Annie crossed her arms. "I'm definitely coming then, to keep you out of trouble. How are we getting there?"

"Jeff will drive us. You're the ideal person to come with me because Dannie's too young. Izzy's too famous. Lynn would stick out like a sore thumb with her psychic look and you've kept yourself out of the newspapers."

"Izzy knows better than to put me in the public eye," she said.

"Exactly, I'm less likely to get recognised if I'm with you."

"I'm regretting this already."

"Nonsense. It'll be a fun night out." I grinned at her. "Don't worry, I'll ask Jeff to wait outside for us, so if any issues arise, we can get out of there, sharpish."

"But if this guy is some sort of crook, he'll find us."

"You're letting your imagination get the better of you. It's a night out."

Her eyes widened. "What do I need to wear?" she asked. "Please don't tell me I have to wear a dress."

I looked her up and down. Annie loved her denim, and I'd never seen her in an occasion dress as she didn't care for the sort of events that required them. "Well, you have seen casinos in spy films, right?"

She spread out her arms. "This is me. I don't like cocktail dresses. And I'd never fit into yours. I've got a couple of sun dresses, that's it."

Looking down at myself, I wondered whether I'd still fit into my dresses myself. I looked back up. "You haven't got one formal dress?"

She bit the inside of her lip.

"Come on, I can see it in your eyes. You have, haven't you?"

"I was a bridesmaid for my cousin."

"What's the dress like?"

"I don't think it's appropriate."

I pulled her towards the back door. "Come on, I'll walk you back and have a look."

Annie lived a couple of doors up from the spiritualist hut, so we went out the back way, through the gate and alongside the hut until we reached the path to her place. Constance trotted ahead of us, illuminated by the streetlamps.

Annie's apartment was on the top floor of the three-story conversion. She let us in and gestured towards a door. "It's in the spare room." Annie sounded as unenthusiastic as you can get.

I turned on the light and opened the mirrored wardrobe door.

"It's gold," she said with a sigh.

The dress was easy to find as it stood out from her other clothes. I pulled it out. "Wow, try it on."

"No, I'll just hold it up against me."

It was an off the shoulder satin number and straight to the floor.

"It looks amazing. What shoes are you going to wear with it?"

She huffed. "I have the gold sandals I wore to the wedding. Now, are you sure I won't look overdressed?"

"Of course not. As Grandma used to say. You can never be overdressed."

THE FOLLOWING EVENING, we walked along the Bristol harbour-side. I wore Grandma's black evening dress, with a jewelled neckline, which fit a lot snugger than it did the last time I wore it. Not that it looked bad, as I seemed to have adopted more of an hourglass figure. Well, maybe not an hour, as such, with me being short. More like a four-minute egg timer. Although, I felt taller in my heels and confidence oozed out of me as the casino came into sight. The actor inside of me rose to the top and five years of performing arts training fired up as I got into character.

Annie, however, appeared less comfortable and had nearly twisted her ankle twice in her gold sandals, which weren't even that high. "Urgh," she said. "The things I have to do to fit in."

"It's nice to dress up once in a while," I said.

"Really? Walking the street on stilts in the evening breeze in this fussy dress with only a thin scarf to cover my shoulders, is not my idea of fun."

"It's called a pashmina," I said. "Hey, stop a minute." I placed my hand on her forearm. "You look amazing. Jeff was blown away when he saw you. Even Constance purred."

"That was the equivalent of a cat chuckle. And Jeff thought I looked silly. I can tell." A gold metal hair band kept her hair from her face. She looked like royalty. A total beauty.

"Well, here we are. Slap on a smile. We're undercover." I took her arm and led her inside. The reception was dark and packed out with an array of huge, fake plants. Fluorescent strip lights lined the edges of the ceiling. I caught my reflection in a mirrored wall. I'd sleeked my hair into a low bun and gelled it to my head. I was sure no-one would recognise me without my usual free-flowing red locks. And so what if they did? If anyone asked, I'd say I was out flashing the cash I'd earned from my previous investigation. It was a free country, and I was out having fun.

"Ladies," the bouncer said, looking us up and down.

We strode passed, and I gave him my best aloof smile.

"That guy smirked at us as if we're idiots," Annie hissed from behind me.

"No, Annie. He was smiling in appraisal because we look amazing."

We reached the cloakroom and passed over our pashminas. Annie took the tickets and placed them in the occasion bag I'd lent her. Next, we visited the cashier and I ordered some chips.

Annie took a deep breath before we opened the door. "I hope I don't regret this."

The main room was a hive of activity. I stopped and gulped. No one appeared to be dressed for a casino. I noticed a few people look in our direction, then some more.

"I thought you said we'd fit in," Annie hissed from my side.

I spoke to her through a wide grin. "Just act cool, as if you belong here."

"But they look like they've come straight from work. It's all suits. Did you check the dress code?"

"Let's just get to a table," I said in a breezy voice.

"I don't believe it. You didn't, did you?"

Around the room, playing various games, people cheered and others groaned. Some winners, more losers. In the corner was a batch of slot machines with a couple of people sat on high stools. The bar ran along the left side with a guy mixing cocktails.

"This is so exciting," I said to Annie.

"Let's get on with it," she said. "What are we playing first?"

"The roulette," I pointed. "The table in the centre, so I can scan the room."

I looked around for Connor Davies. There was no sign of his white dinner jacket. Maybe he only wore that outfit for the cameras. He was the reason I'd assumed the dress code was DJ's and cocktail dresses."

We found a table with two spare chairs together. The other players were two middle-aged couples and a pair of young guys who were more than a little drunk.

"Woah, love," slurred a guy to Annie. "Have you just come from a wedding?"

I avoided making eye contact with Annie. I just put out my hand, so she didn't take off.

"You look amazing girls," his less drunk companion said. "But this table isn't lucky tonight."

The drunk guy stood up. "I'll get more chips." He staggered away, bumping into chairs as he went.

"Place your bets, please," the croupier said.

Annie smiled at him, then spoke under her breath. "Now he's my type of man."

I gently dug her in the ribs with my elbow. "We're on a job, not on the pull."

She had a point, though, the croupier was good-looking with a chiselled jaw, gorgeous eyes and a face and physique that wouldn't look out of place on the front of a men's health magazine.

"Let's go red or black," I said to Annie as she continued to smile across the table at the croupier.

I placed a five-pound chip on red and we watched the roulette spin. The ball bounced around before landing on five.

"Yes," Annie said. "We won."

The croupier gave her a small smile and passed her a card to track our progress. "This helps if you're playing a black or red game," he said in a deep, velvety voice.

"Thanks," Annie said, then whispered to me. "For a moment there, I thought he was passing me his number." She fanned herself with the score card.

I'd never been for a night out with Annie before. I was seeing a different side to her. "Will you please concentrate? We're looking for Connor." I snatched the card from her, grabbed a pen and marked up our win.

The drunk guy returned to the table, and we bet another five-pound chip. This time, we weren't so lucky.

"Better luck next time," said the drunk guy as he leaned forward, his eyelids drooping as if he was just about to pass out.

"Someone's going to make a mint out of us tonight," I said to his less drunk friend.

"Yeah, and he doesn't need it neither," he said.

"Who's the owner?" I asked. *May as well get on with it.*

Annie placed her chin in her hand, blatantly giving the croupier the eye. I was seeing her in a whole new light.

"Connor Davies," he said. "He's over at the blackjack table." He gestured across the room. "He plays every night."

I glanced to where he was pointing and soon spotted the white dinner jacket. "What's he like?" I asked.

"I'll introduce you."

"No, need for that," I said.

He stood up. "Come on, I'm a regular." He laughed. "Although I can't promise he won't bite."

"Annie. Annie," I said, trying to get her attention. "We're going over to the blackjack table."

"In a minute." She shooed me away with her hand and she placed a chip on fifteen. "I'll just finish here." She flashed another big smile across the table.

I walked across the room with the man. As we got closer, I saw Connor was sitting next to a woman with chestnut hair swept up in a ponytail. He smiled at her and put his hand under her chin then gave her a hug. *She looks just like …*

The woman pulled away laughing and then turned to the side.

I recognised the profile instantly … *Tara.* "Actually," I said to the man. "I need the powder room first. Could you point me in the right direction?"

"It's over there," he said, nodding to the ladies sign.

I looked back to Connor Davies, and as I did, Tara turned around. We locked eyes. *Oh dear,* I thought, giving a quick smile before heading for the toilet. Once inside the ladies' room, I went inside the nearest cubicle and fished my phone out of my bag. I texted Annie:

URGENT Tara is here with Connor Davies. My hand shook as I tapped at the screen. *I'm in the loo. Come find me.*

I gulped. What did this mean? H's girlfriend cozied up with a dodgy casino owner? One who had a reputation for bumping people off? I heard the toilet door open. I guessed it was Annie.

I yanked open the cubicle door. "Annie," I said, then stopped. It wasn't her.

"Becky." Tara stared down at me from what must have been more than a six-foot height with the killer heels she wore.

"Fancy seeing you here," I said as I rubbed the front of my neck. Losing every iota of my actress bravado.

"What are you doing?" Tara clearly wasn't one for small talk.

"I'm just about to wash my hands." I gave a short laugh.

"At the casino. Why are you here? And what's with the dress? It's not James Bond, you know."

"Last night Annie and me were played poker with H." I paused and raised my eyebrows. "We decided to give it a whirl in the real world." I could feel the heat rising up my neck.

"Do you think I was born yesterday?"

"What do you mean?"

"You followed me here, didn't you?" She tapped her foot.

"What? No." I shook my head. "Honestly, I didn't." That was the truth.

She sighed. "You're no doubt doing another one of your silly investigations."

How dare she. "I've been successful in the past." I took a deep breath. *Don't let her wind you up.*

She shook her head. "That's not how I heard it. You interfere where you don't belong and H rescues you." She looked at her reflection in the mirror and pulled a lipstick from her bag.

"That's not true. Is that what he told you?" I put my hands on my hips.

She gave me a small smirk via the mirror. "I know you followed me."

"I had absolutely no idea you were here." I looked towards the door. "But seeing as you are." I gestured at her. "What are you doing here?"

Tara swiped a flash of red across her lips, then sighed. Her face became serious. "Be careful, Becky. I'm warning you. You could get hurt." She put her lipstick in her bag and turned to face me.

"Are you threatening me?" I swallowed hard but didn't want her to think I was afraid of her – even if she was staring me out.

She took a step backwards. "Of course not. But go home, it's not a game." Then left the room, banging the door behind her.

I let out a long breath and then glanced at my totally crimson reflection before leaving the room as well. I looked across at Annie, she was seated as close to the croupier as she could possibly get. Seemingly oblivious of the world around her. I glanced across the room and saw Tara disappearing through a door with *V.I.P.* written on it.

"Here's the beautiful lady."

I swung around to find the guy we'd being playing roulette with staring at me. Behind him was Connor Davies.

"Hi," I squeaked.

Up close, Connor was attractive in a Bond-villain kind of way. His white-blond hair was neat, and he had a scar on his left cheek. He gave me a smile, warm yet menacing.

I gulped.

His blue eyes were nearly see-through, giving him an even more of a movie-villain vibe. He put out his hand.

"Pleased to meet you," I said. My hands were sweating, so I decided not to shake his and opted for a little wave instead.

"I hear you've had bad luck at the table?" he said. His voice was thick with the local Bristol accent.

"Oh, I only lost a little. It's my first time."

He took my hand, then lifted it to his mouth before planting a kiss. "I don't want you to spend all of that reward you received for recovering the diamonds."

Okay, cover blown. I guessed Tara had filled him in on who I was.

"Maybe I can guide you through your next game?"

He squeezed my hand, and I cringed. He must have been able to feel how hot it was.

I gave a laugh so nervous I sounded like a bleating goat. "I've had a great evening, but I'd better be going now," I said. "My friend is tired." I nodded in Annie's direction as she threw her head back and laughed.

"She looks more than fine to me. And you're both stunning." He lifted my hand and twirled me around. I just about kept my balance until he caught me with his arm tight around my waist, so close I felt as if we were just about to dance the Argentine Tango.

"This is how I would like all the guests to dress here," he said into my ear as he squeezed my waist. "I'm so pleased you came. Please, join me for a drink. Anything you want is on the house."

I tried to pull away, but he was having none of it and the guy from the roulette table had disappeared. "I think I need to go home."

"I've just the thing to wake you up, my beauty." Connor released me and put his hand on the small of my back. "This way, I have a V.I.P. lounge." He guided me across the room towards the door that Tara had walked through. "I've read all about you. You're so much more beautiful in the flesh."

I could agree with him there, considering many of the photos of me in the newspaper had caught me in a string of unflattering poses. My heart thudded. Tara had told me to go home. But she also appeared to have dropped me in it. Just wait until I told H that she was two-timing him with crooked Connor, like a double agent. I disliked the woman before, but at that moment, I detested her.

I turned around before we went through the door to see Annie scanning the room, looking worried. She caught my eye just as Connor swept me through the door. We travelled along a mirror-lined corridor, heading towards the V.I.P. bar. Once inside, there were a few people sitting in booths with a couple of waitresses, wearing not an awful lot, carrying trays of drinks.

As we got closer to the bar, I saw a familiar face on top of a huge bulk scowling at me. My heart pounded. *Bad Cop Brad.* I wasn't sure if I was relieved or petrified to see the D.C.I. With so much adrenalin coursing through my body, it was difficult to tell.

Conner removed his hand from my back and approached him. "Ah, Detective Chief Inspector, what would you like to drink?"

Brad glowered at me, then faced Connor. "I need a word. In private."

Connor turned to me. "I'll see you at that booth." He pointed to a booth with a gold voile curtain.

I scanned the room for Tara.

A waitress approached. "Can I help?"

"I'm waiting for Connor," I said, nodding at him and Brad at the end of the bar, then looked back at the exit. Tara was right, I needed to get out of that place. I felt my ears burn as Brad nodded in my direction as he spoke to Connor.

"There you are," Annie said from behind me in a

puffed-out voice. She had our pashminas in her hand. "We need to go. Now."

She looked over my shoulder and her eyes widened.

"Becky, thanks for waiting."

I spun around to find Connor smiling at me. He turned to the waitress. "Open a bottle of Dom Perignon, Katie."

"Unfortunately, we can't stay," Annie said, putting herself between Connor and me.

I was glad I'd brought her and not Izzy. She would have been lapping it up.

"I'm sure we can spend another half hour together." Connor sidestepped Annie and grabbed my hand. Pulling me towards him.

Annie stepped back and put a hand on her left hip. "I've called the chauffeur. He's waiting on double yellows."

Connor reached into his pocket. "It seems you're being whisked away." He passed me his card. "Here are my numbers. I'd love to see you again."

I took the card with a relieved smile and channelled my most sophisticated self. "Thank you, Mr Davies, you're so sweet."

He snaked both arms around my waist and pulled me close so I could barely breathe. Before I could lean away, he landed a kiss bang on my lips. As he released me, I laughed nervously and looked around. Tara was standing a few feet away, with fiery eyes.

Annie took my hand and marched me out. "You'll

get yourself killed at this rate," she said in a loud whisper as she dragged me through the door.

I turned and saw Bad Cop Brad following. "Yep. Let's get out of here, quick."

Outside, we climbed into the van, which stunk of burger and fries.

"Drive," I said, putting on my seatbelt as I looked for any sign of Bad Cop Brad. But he hadn't followed us out. That was a relief. Even so, I wasn't looking forward to bumping into him again.

Jeff finished a mouthful of food before speaking. "You were quick."

I filled him in on what had happened as Constance jumped onto my lap.

"Wait, what?" Jeff said as he swung the van onto the main road home. "Tara is having a romance with crooked Connor?"

"He had his arm around her, put his hand under her chin and gave her a huge hug. They didn't snog," I said.

"Unlike you and him," Annie said.

"I did not. He gave me nowhere to go."

"Boss, you kissed a suspect?" Jeff asked.

"She's exaggerating," I wound the window down a little, to try and get rid of the burger-gherkin smell.

"But you could tell Tara and Connor were close, for sure," Annie said

"Yeah, really close. Maybe she would do anything for him," I said.

"Like kill a rival?" Jeff gave a low whistle. "That's insane."

"Yes," I said, firmly placing Tara at the top of my list of suspects. I can't lie, it felt good. "She warned me off as well. Near threatened me. Saying I'd get hurt."

Constance gave a low wail.

"Don't worry, I'm fine." I scratched her head. "Annie, meanwhile, was cosying up to the croupier while I was battling with the enemy."

"I'll have you know. I was finding out information."

"Like what?" I asked.

"I was asking Wes about Eddie Fly."

"And? What did he say?"

"He said he'd seen him there."

"Is that it? I bet the only information you got from him was his phone number."

"I did not," she said as her phone buzzed with a message.

"Of course not." I shook my head.

"I may have added him on Snapchat." She checked her phone, and we had a couple of quiet minutes, apart from the odd giggle from Annie.

Jeff broke the silence as we passed the *Welcome to Branden Bay* sign. "What are you going to say to H?"

Annie looked at the clock on Jeff's dash. "I'll come back to yours and we can have a think of how to approach it. It's a very delicate situation. Whether he's serious with Tara or not, he's clearly close to the woman and she's very close with another man."

"Who's a crook." Jeff gave a low whistle.

"I'm not liking it, Annie," I said. "Why would a woman go out with a known criminal and a policeman at the same time?" I shook my head. "It screams scandal to me. I told you I didn't like her. I wonder if Bad Cop Brad saw her there too?" I asked. "Maybe he was tailing her? Seeing as she's a suspect."

"That's a point," Annie said. "I think H is going to want to hear about it from his friends rather than D.C.I. Harris."

We drove back, chatting some more, until we reached Beach Road. As Jeff slowed the van, we saw that H's car was parked up outside my house.

"Oh. I think he's already heard," I said.

CHAPTER 15

H's voice boomed at us as we entered the house. "What are you playing at?"

Constance trotted over to him and rubbed herself up against his shin as if she was attempting to calm him down. I'd never seen him so angry.

"And what's with the clothes?" He gestured at Annie. "You look like a Christmas cracker."

"Thanks for that," Annie said, slamming her bag on the hall table.

Dannie called from behind him. "I'll get the kettle on." She hurried away.

Marcus walked down the staircase. "What's going on?"

I looked from Marcus to H and crossed my arms. "We went to the casino."

"I know exactly where you've been," H said, pointing at me and then turned to Annie. "I can't believe you encouraged her, you're the most sensible person I know."

"Calm down," Annie said. "You said last night I'd be great at the blackjack table."

"I've had Tara on the phone in tears, saying that you've been stalking her."

I put my hands on my hips. "Crocodile tears more like. And that's rubbish, we didn't know she'd be there."

"Becky's right. We were shocked to see her." Annie raised her eyebrows at me. "Let's calm down and have that cup of tea Dannie's making. Then we can talk sensibly about this."

Tara was clearly trying to discredit us before we spilled the beans and judging by H's reaction – it was working. As much as I wanted to tell him to get out of the house for the way he was trying to push me around, I needed to get the information across to him that his girlfriend was mixed up with a gangster.

Jeff and Marcus remained silent as they watched the confrontation.

I took a deep breath and picked Constance up and walked into the café via the internal door.

H followed and as soon as he was inside, closed the door behind us to prevent the others following. "You tailed Tara to Bristol as part of your so-called investigation. Go on admit it."

I swung around with my cat still in my arms. "Honestly, we didn't," I said as I placed Constance on the floor, who meowed loudly.

"I don't know who you think you are but going off mixing with a dangerous man and kissing him is not cool, Becky."

"I ... I didn't." *Tara really has filled him in,* I thought. "Look, let's sit down," I said taking a seat at a table.

H lowered his voice. "I also had a call from Brad. I won't repeat his exact words, but he made it plain and simple. Keep out of it. There'll be no more warnings. He'll arrest you on the spot." He sat down. "Look, I know you think you're doing something for the greater good, but you could get hurt. It's only because I care about you." He ran a hand through his hair. "And Connor Davies? You really kissed him?"

As he looked into my eyes, I felt his anger subside but the look in his face suggested it had been replaced with worry. I stood up. "'I'll fetch the tea and cake"

THE SIX OF us sat at a large café table in silence, drinking tea and eating cake. Marcus and H scowled at each other. Dannie yawned and kept glancing at the clock, clearly wishing she was in bed. Jeff sat wide-eyed and Annie was glued to her phone with a faraway look in her eyes. Constance purred as H stroked her.

Annie looked up and mouthed at me. "Tell him."

It seemed mean to say Tara was all over Connor. She was obviously trying to cover it up by saying I was snogging the guy. I decided to explain why we were there instead. "I visited Fiona Fly and she said that Eddie had trodden on the toes of Connor Davies. So we went to the casino to get a look at him. I didn't plan to speak to him."

H let out a long breath. "Davies is serious gangland, that's why Brad is on the case. He's well known to the Vice Squad and has been living under the radar for years. The police have never caught him with his hands dirty. A few of his enemies have disappeared. They found one employee floating in the harbour." His eyes swept the room. "I'm telling you as a friend, you all need to stop pursuing this case."

"That's easy for you to say. You're not the one with an uninvited guest," I said.

"Hey, that's a bit below the belt," Marcus said.

I hadn't been referring to him. I'd been talking about Eddie's ghost, but I didn't correct Marcus. After all, I wanted him to leave as well.

"You're not an investigator, Becky, you're a baker. Just leave it," H said.

"Stop having a go at me, as if I'm the one that's in the wrong. There's something you need to know." I realised there was no going back now.

H sat back in his chair. "Let's have it then."

I exchanged a look with Annie who gave me a slow nod.

"Tara and Connor appeared to be close. Like really close."

Jeff looked down at his hands, as if he thought H was going to blow.

H slowly shook his head and as he did, he saw the

A-Frame in the corner of the room. "What's that?" He gestured towards it.

"Nothing," I said as he stood up.

He approached the make-shift murder board. I groaned as he reached it.

"What the ...?" he said as he pointed at it. "I'm on your suspect list?" He shook his head. "Maybe you'd like to talk me through this?"

"I, er ..." There was no getting out of it. I stood up, lifted my dress, as I'd already kicked off my stilettos, and walked over to my murder board. "Okay. First, we have Marcus here, who you think did it."

"You do?" Marcus asked H.

H ignored him.

"Then we have everyone else in Corelli's that night. Councillor Levison and his wife Gina, Fiona Fly, Elena Corelli, Frank DuPont, Molly O'Brien and Tara. We still need to add Connor Davies." I picked a marker from the side and wrote 'Connor Davies' on the board, then drew a new red line from his name to Tara." I put the marker down and put a hand on my hip. "There's a link between Tara and the murder weapon and between Tara and someone who had threatened Eddie's life."

H clapped his hands slowly. "Well done. What do you specialise in again? Cupcakes?"

I clenched my teeth.

H gestured at the board. "I see you've missed off Tara's surname." He picked the pen up from the table and wrote a name next to Tara. *Davies*. "Tara is Connor's younger sister."

"Oh." I looked at Annie.

"Whoops." She looked back at H.

"So, she's part of a gangster family?" I asked him.

H pointed at us all. "Get to bed and forget this case. I'm well aware who Tara is. She's done nothing wrong. She's been distancing herself from Connor and got herself a job outside of the family business. She's come to Branden Bay for a fresh start. I suggest you stop pointing the finger at a woman trying to grab herself a new life and allow the police to focus on the prime suspect." He nodded at Marcus.

"Hey, I'm innocent." Marcus stood up. "You've got to ask yourself, man. What's a crooked millionaire casino owner's sister doing teaching keep fit lessons in a back-water place like this? Seems to me she's playing a long game. And you've swallowed it, mate. Getting to know the local copper with a turning-over-a-new-leaf sob story, then wham, hits her prey where it hurts." He looked at me. "Well, in the neck, with a knife."

I frowned and crossed my arms. I wanted to be the one to say all of that. Marcus had sucked the lines right out of me. "He has a point," I said.

"Tara has a rock-solid alibi. She was with me." H thumped his swelled chest. "I drove her home that night and went inside her place for coffee."

"I bet you did," Marcus said. "She's one hot bird."

"Before coming back to Branden Bay and receiving your call," H said, ignoring Marcus and looking at me.

I felt the colour rise to my face.

H shook his head at me. "Stay out of it, Becky, else you'll wind up in the cells again. Or worse, floating in Bristol harbour." He pointed at Annie. "And you, don't encouraging her."

Annie remained silent, as did Jeff and Dannie, although Constance gave a low meow.

H turned back to me. "I'm off to Devon at dawn. Keep out of it because I won't be here to save your backside next time."

DRINKING my morning cuppa in the kitchen, I stared at the murder board. I stretched out my back, having slept on the sofa in the snug. As awkward as it was sleeping on a two-seater sofa, I'd had enough of my night-time fix of Eddie's murder. I felt drained and was well aware that I needed to solve this mystery to get rid of Eddie and Marcus for good. A normal life seemed like utter bliss. Constance jumped onto my lap and snuggled down. I always felt much calmer when she was close by.

"Alright boss?"

I turned to see Jeff in the doorway. "I'm trying to get everything straight in my head."

"Want to talk it through?" he asked looking at the murder board before taking a seat next to me.

"I keep going around in circles with it. I feel we should go over to the Budget Inn where the knife turned up, to see if I can pick up any vibes. Use the so-called psychic powers I've been given."

"Great idea. I knock off work at four."

LATER, we climbed out of the van and approached the Budget Inn reception. I smelled curry wafting from their canteen-style restaurant. I doubted it was the tastiest example of Indian cuisine, but my stomach still rumbled. We opened the door.

As we walked in, the young woman on the desk looked up and her eyes widened. "You're the paranormal investigators."

I nodded and smiled. *No point denying it.* "I'm Becky."

She grinned. "And you're Jeff." She fluttered her eyelashes at him.

I raised my eyebrows and looked at Jeff, who stood mouth agape.

"Are you here about the ..." she lowered her voice, "knife?"

I nodded.

"Have the police asked you to help with the case?"

Now, I should have said no, and I saw a picture of Brad flash into my mind. But still – I nodded. I mean, without saying the actual word 'yes', was it even a proper lie?

"The cleaner found it in the corner of the car park." She pointed out of the window to where it had been located. "It was in a plastic bag."

"Did you see anyone lurking around or displaying any strange behaviour?"

She shrugged. "I haven't really thought about it. Everyone said it was that bloke you knew from London that done it. The one they arrested. Wait ... isn't it him?"

"It doesn't look like it," I said. "So we're widening the net."

"I guess you want the full guest list, then?"

This was going well. I hadn't come in for that, but maybe it would be useful. "I don't need to take it, but if I could have a quick look?"

"Sure." She opened the bookings programme.

I leaned over, peering at the screen.

"Oh, have you got a warrant?"

"No," Jeff said. "It can take a while to come through."

"I'd better check with my line manager. We had some data protection training the other day, and I don't want to get into any trouble." She got up and left via a door behind her, but didn't close her screen.

"They're never going to give it to us, boss." Jeff rubbed his growing beard.

"I know that." I snuck behind the desk. Having worked on reception myself, I was completely familiar with booking systems. At least the three years at the city firm were paying off. I flicked to the sixth of August. Running my eyes along the page, I pulled my phone out and took pictures. "There are loads of names here. Keep a lookout."

After snapping a few shots, I heard movement behind me and dropped to the floor. "I lost my bracelet," I said as I stood up.

The manager glared at me. "Can I help?" she asked. "I understand you're working for the police?"

"No, not at all," I said, throwing an apologetic look at the receptionist.

"I'm sure I don't need to explain that we do not give out sensitive information to amateur sleuths. Certainly not those pedalling nonsense about ghosts."

"Of course not. I'm sorry to have bothered you." I grabbed Jeff by the arm and went outside.

"Did you get anything?" he asked me.

"I snapped a few pictures of the guest list. Come on, let's sit here." I pointed to a bench.

I pulled the pictures up on my phone and spent a few minutes scanning the names. "Aha. There's an O'Brien."

"Molly O'Brien?" asked Jeff.

I nodded. "A Miss M O'Brien," I said as a black SUV drew up. "Oh, no." It screeched to a stop in front of us and the door burst open. I knew who to expect. *Bad Cop Brad.*

Once out he opened the rear door and pointed at me, then back at the car. "In."

Jeff sat rooted to the spot.

I pushed my phone into my back pocket. There was no time to delete the evidence. I entered the car and Brad took the front seat.

"We've had a complaint that you stole information

from the Budget Inn. You're looking at a possible custo-dial sentence for that."

I swallowed hard. "I'm just trying to clear Marcus's name."

"I've dealt with drug dealers, sex traffickers, murderers ..."

"Yes, you're an award-winning cop. I know, I've seen the medal." I didn't mean for it to sound sarcastic. I was merely stating a fact, but by the look on Brad's face as he turned around and glared at me, I guessed it came out that way.

He turned on the engine. "I'm taking you in."

"No, wait. I've got loads to do. It's the Victorian Town Theme Day tomorrow."

He drove me towards the station, speeding like it was the formula one.

"Hey, I haven't even got my seatbelt on," I shouted over the sound of the engine. I held onto the back of the driver's seat. "I want Marcus out of town. If you hadn't told him to stay in Branden Bay, trust me, I wouldn't have bothered. I don't want him in my house. I think I know who did it."

Brad screeched the car to a halt. My head bashed against the headrest in front. I sat back rubbing it, wondering whether a complaint would get Brad the sack.

He didn't look at me but yelled out. "Speak."

"Molly O'Brien was waitressing at Corelli's and stayed at the Budget Inn where the weapon was found. She was upset with Eddie. She said to Elena Corelli that Eddie had no heart. She clearly knew him. She had access to steak knives. And..." I paused. I'd not told Brad about my vision.

"And what?" he growled.

"I had a vision of Eddie's death and H drove me up to Millar's, that night."

"Not that load of –"

"Hear me out. While I was waiting in the car, I saw a woman hiding in a shop doorway. She ran off when more police arrived, it could have been Molly. Have you interviewed her yet?"

"I don't answer to you, James. I'm taking you in, where I'll read you your rights and charge you. I'll give you a date to return to the police station for formal questioning at which time you need to bring your lawyer. You may well blind D.S. Blake, but I'm not falling for your hapless charms and you won't be involved in any future investigations. Do you understand?"

I gulped. I really was in a lot of trouble this time. But at least I'd given him a lead, and hopefully he'd move on to Molly and I'd get shot of Marcus.

"Put your seatbelt on." He sped away as soon as it clicked into place.

WHEN I RETURNED HOME LATER, I was totally drained. I'd been at the police station for two hours. And now there was a tonne of baking to do for the Victorian Town Theme Day. I literally had to stay up all night baking. I couldn't ask Lynn to do it as she would need to be wide awake for the day in case I fell asleep on the job. Sniffing back the tears, I made up scone mix and sponge batter. Constance rubbed herself up against me, staying by my side until I finished in the early hours of the morning.

CHAPTER 16

I sat in the snug, stroking Constance as I sipped my morning tea. The sun shone as I gazed out to the lush garden. But I had to admit, I was missing H. Not that I saw him that often, but knowing he was in another county did not sit well with me. It was surprising, considering I'd spent months thinking I didn't even like the guy. Reeling from his telling off about Tara, I couldn't call or text him, as I'd have to tell him about my run in with Brad. Mind you, his sister, Rachael, would probably tell him anyway since I'd had to call her for legal help. I was due up at the police station in three days.

Marcus had been helping around the café in out of the way jobs such as taking the rubbish out and washing up. I saw a change in him and, at times, forgot he was the same Marcus I'd spent three years with. His arrogance was replaced by someone who genuinely wanted to be of help. He had also laid off with the old 'are we getting back together' chat. I left Constance snuggled asleep on the sofa and found Marcus in the kitchen making a hot drink.

"I want to help with the Victorian Town Theme Day," he said. "My parents are coming to town tomorrow and I need something to take my mind off it."

"You're not bringing them here, are you?" The last thing I wanted to do was face that pair.

"No, I'm meeting them in the pub along the seafront. It would have been Millar's but well ... it'd be a bit awkward with the staff thinking I committed a murder there."

"You could help with the baking," I suggested. "I've mixed all of the dough and batters." I left him instructions and, after checking on him a couple of times, was surprised at how industrious he was. There were neat groups of baked scones and cookies.

In the café, I found Lynn and Jeff wearing the white Victorian baker outfits I'd bought.

Lynn laughed. "We look like The Bun Family out of that Happy Families card game." She was right, especially Jeff, with his brown flat cap.

"Shall we go up for the official ribbon cutting before we open?" I said. "Marcus can hold the fort in the kitchen."

"That's a marvellous idea," Lynn said.

Once outside, we passed the cart I'd hired to wheel our bakes around to sell. The streets were empty of visitors. Traders had set up stalls along the prom. I felt a lump form in my throat. Having become so close to this town, I was proud of what we'd collectively achieved. I just hoped the visitors would turn up to make it a success.

We reached the foot of the High Street, where a stage was set up. Councillor Levison was upon it, with his wife Gina by his side. She didn't look as full of life as she had in the restaurant, her face was drawn and her mouth downcast. Beside her were Andrew, Katherine and Annie who had a fake grin. She wasn't one for soaking up this much attention especially when she was wearing a full length Victorian dress. The High Street was so packed, it reminded me of The Mall on the day of a royal wedding. Izzy stood to the side of the platform in a cordoned-off area with a photographer from the Gazette.

Levison tapped the microphone and addressed the audience. "Good morning and welcome to Branden Bay."

The crowd applauded. Levison waited for the clapping and whistling to subside. "So much work has gone into the planning of today," he said. "It was the brainchild of Andrew Farr, who has been working tirelessly with the Council to protect and preserve the Victorian charm of ..." He looked at Andrew, "our town."

The crowd cheered some more.

"And I'd like to thank others for their support, such as Katherine Sheringham, the staff of the pier and fairground and of course the many local businesspeople who have pulled together as a team, to make this happen."

Lynn nudged me and smiled like a proud parent.

Levison continued. "And the volunteers who have stepped forward to make the day a special one."

"It's going to be insane," Jeff said.

"I'll make it short," Levison said as he stepped down from the stage and approached the ribbon held taught across the road by a couple of volunteers. "As I know you're all excited about exploring the themed town. I hereby announce Branden Bay's Victorian Town Theme Day, open." He cut the yellow ribbon.

"We'd better get back quick," I said.

We hurried back to the café, ahead of the crowd as if we were being chased by a wave up the beach.

Dannie was out the front, loading up the cart with fresh bakes. They looked tempting and I was sure we'd sell out. Once inside, Lynn fired up the commercial coffee machine.

I found Marcus in the kitchen.

"You've got an actual production line going on," I said. "I'll show you how to make up the mixes because it's heaving out there. I've got the supplies but it will mean you'll be out here for a lot of the day.

"That's good with me. I'm enjoying it. It takes my mind off things."

I nodded. "I'd love to focus on baking instead of being interrupted by murders." I scribbled out the recipes for the cookies and scones.

"You better get out there," he said.

As I went to help Lynn with the orders, I heard someone call my name.

"Becky." It was Fiona Fly standing in the queue.

"Come here," I said ushering her in. "Lynn," I called out. "This is Fiona. Whatever she wants is on the house." I turned back to her. "I'll come over and see you once I've seated everyone and taken orders."

Lynn and I were rushed off our feet. It was as if a whole trainload of visitors decided they would start the day with tea and cake. Not that I was complaining, the till would be full.

"Phew," I said as I sat down with Fiona once all the tables were filled. "How are you?"

"I'm holding up. They've not released Eddie's body, so I can't do a funeral yet. But I need some sort of closure, so we'll have a memorial service. It'll be at church because he was a religious man."

"So I understand. Marcus slipped over on a set of rosary beads in the hotel room."

Fiona frowned. "No, he wasn't that sort of Christian. He was more of a born again. Not that I ever went. All jeans, he said, and not a robe in sight. Anyway, the reason I popped in was to say that I remembered where I'd seen that girl before. She's Connor Davies's sister. She usually has her hair up in a ponytail so didn't recognise her that night in the restaurant. I'll be telling the police."

"They already know," I said. "I since found out, she was related to Connor."

"You really are good. Do you think she could have murdered Eddie for her brother?"

"She has an alibi." I pushed away the picture in my mind of H snuggled up and smooching with Tara on her sofa. "It's not her."

"She may have taken the knife though, passed it to one of his goons and framed Marcus."

I frowned, I hadn't thought of that angle. *Maybe I should stick her back on the murder board?* I wondered whether Brad Cop Brad had called Molly in after I'd given him the tip off about her connection to Eddie and the Budget Inn where the knife was found.

"Did you remember where you knew Molly from? The waitress?" I asked.

Fiona ran a hand through her hair. "Now you've mentioned her name. It does ring a bell. She may have worked for Ed or something."

I guessed Fiona knew exactly who Molly was, she just didn't want any indication that her marriage had been on the rocks, as Marcus had indicated.

Lynn placed a tea and cookie in front of Fiona.

Fiona looked up at her. "Thank you." Then turned to me. "Did you visit Connor Davies?"

I nodded. "You were right, he's one dodgy guy. Charismatic though." I smiled.

"Do you think he had something to do with it?"

"I don't know." I didn't want to be the one answering the questions and I was busy. I could under-stand Fiona taking an interest. After all, her husband was the one that had been murdered.

"So how are you progressing with your investigation?" she said then took a sip of her tea.

"I'm getting there," I said, not adding any details, Fiona wasn't my client. I wanted to pursue this case for myself. I didn't have to divulge anything to this woman.

Fiona looked out of the café doors then flushed. "Right, I'll be off now to have a mooch around." She wrapped her cookie up in a serviette and stood up. "It's been so nice to see you. I hope this matter is solved soon so I can get on with the rest of my life."

I watched her go, pushing her way through the crowd in the direction of the prom until she reached a guy. His body was masked by the crowd but I could see he was wearing a tweed flat cap. *I wonder who that is?* I thought. A shot of static passed through my body. Something was afoot. I felt a nudge to follow Fiona and her companion. I loaded up a bag of extra cookies. "I'm going to find Jeff and replenish the cart," I called out to Lynn as Constance followed me out of the door.

I picked Constance up as I passed the stalls, fearing she would become lost amongst the sea of legs and wished I'd left her back at the café. Carrying her and the cookies was quite a load. The fresh smells from the food stalls were amazing. I wasn't sure that all the food was strictly Victorian themed, but the crowds were loving it. I was impressed by the amount of people who had come dressed up as well. I even spotted a whole family wearing striped Victorian bathing suits. It was busier than I could ever remember. I scanned the prom but saw no sign of Fiona. I looked around for Jeff realising he could be anywhere. I heard singing and made my way to a stage set up on the beach next to the pier. A children's choir sang. I plonked myself down on a deckchair, which came free, and placed the cookies on my lap as Constance sat out of the sun, underneath the deckchair. She seemed quite hot in the sunny weather, which wasn't surprising considering her bushy coat. The kids were from Branden Bay Primary School and they sang traditional songs. I hummed along until the tune changed to *Cockles and Mussels.* My blood ran cold as they sang the song, which I now associated with Eddie's gruesome death.

"In Dublin's fair city, where the girls are so pretty, I first set my eyes on sweet Molly Malone ..."

"Molly?" I said to Constance. As they sang, I brought up a picture of Eddie singing the song. At that part of the vison, he'd seemed truly happy. *They were going to meet,* I thought. Maybe he'd arranged for her to come over. A seeping realisation told me Molly was not guilty. What if Fiona had found out about her? "What do you think, Constance?" I looked underneath the deckchair. "Hey, Constance?" She wasn't there. "Constance," I called out. I jumped from the deckchair, scanning the area around me. A little boy eating an ice-cream stared at me, then reached for his mother's hand.

"Connie." It was unlike her not to come when I called. I hunted around some more, it was possible she was being petted by some children. But she was nowhere to be seen. I glanced at my phone, realising I must find Jeff to offload the biscuits and hoped she'd made her way home.

I reached the café within five minutes and saw Jeff's cart parked up outside. I placed the cookies inside it. Dannie was cleaning a table surrounded by eager customer. The place was packed.

"Is Constance here? I can't find her?"

"No, but don't worry. She'll find her way back," Dannie said.

I was sure she was right, but my heart pounded. As the day progressed, I became increasingly tense and my cat didn't show up.

BY BEDTIME, there was still no sign of Constance, and I was in tears. "Something bad has happened, I know it has," I said. I'd spent hours searching for her with my friends, except Izzy, who was working on her piece for the Gazette, but she helped by posting pictures of Constance all over social media asking for people to look out for her.

"I'm sure she's fine." I could tell by Lynn's expression, she was as worried as I was. "Now get some sleep, lovey, you were up all last night baking. Jeff is going out again. Don't worry, he'll find her."

I drifted into a restless sleep. Dreaming of Constance, my wonderful cat, until a shock of static woke me. I sighed. It was probably time for Eddie's haunting like clockwork at half eleven, but when I looked at the clock, it was only ten forty-five. I heard someone gently call my name. I sat up to see the familiar sight of someone I loved.

"Becky." A vision of Grandma stood at the end of my bed. Floating before me as it glowed a purplish pink. "Quick, sugar. The tide is coming in." She disappeared.

I scrambled out of bed and pulled on my jeans before knocking on the other bedroom doors. "Up. Up. Constance is on the beach and the tide is coming in," I called to everyone from the landing. I knew what Grandma meant. She always appeared when Constance was close to spending one of her nine lives.

Once dressed, Jeff, Dannie and Marcus accompanied me out of the house. With flashlights turned on our phones we raced across the carless road, covered in litter and remnants of the day. Hearing the waves charging in, I sped across the prom until I was on the sand.

"Constance! Constance!" I called, squinting as a pinkish purple glow floated underneath the pier. "There." I stumbled across the sand, tripping over, Marcus helped me up as Dannie and Jeff ran ahead of us. A black bag was dangerously close to the water's edge. I heard my cat wailing.

"Get that bag," I screamed.

Dannie reached the bag first, leaning forward for the handles but failed to grab it, Jeff pounded into the frothy surf and scooped up the bag with his long spindly arm. He put it on the sand well away from the water.

Bawling my eyes out, I reached them and unzipped the bag, which had the Millar's logo on it.

I pulled Constance out, she was dripping wet. I buried my face in her salty fur then stuffed her under my top and pressed her close to my warm skin. I could feel her little warm heart beating frantically next to mine. "Bring the bag," I said. "Whoever did this has really crossed the line."

BACK AT THE CAFÉ, I wrapped Constance in a towel and hand-fed her salmon.

"Do you think we should call the police?" Jeff asked as he held up a damp note which said, 'Stop' on it, which he had retrieved from the gym bag.

"I really don't think it's worth it," I said. "They'll only blame me for interfering, and I want to be with Constance, not up at the station."

"The cat-napper obviously wanted you to find her, if there was a message in the bag," Dannie said.

"Maybe they expected her to be washed up on the beach tomorrow morning," Jeff said.

"That's evil," Marcus said. "The poor thing." He gingerly put out his hand and stroked Constance's head.

Constance looked at him sorrowfully, without showing her teeth.

"If H was here …" I trailed off, biting my lip to stop the tears.

Jeff held the note up. "It's something the mob would do. It's in a gym bag."

"Who do we know who is often at Millar's gym?" Marcus said.

I swallowed. "Do you think Tara would do this?"

Lynn placed a hand on my shoulder. "We need to tell H."

"I'll call him," Jeff said.

AT TWO IN THE MORNING, H arrived. "I've only been gone a couple of days."

"I'm sorry," I stuttered.

"It's fine. I was coming back tomorrow anyway to see Ma for Sunday lunch." He put a hand on my shoulder. "Look, I'm sure this was nothing to do with Tara, but I'll speak to her and see if there's any way her brother could be involved, to put your mind at rest."

"Whoever it is, must think I'm getting close to the truth. But I've no idea who killed Eddie. I thought it was Molly, but now I think Eddie still loved her. It's a total mess."

"It's not your mess though, Becky," H said. He put his arm around me.

Marcus hung his head. "Sorry Becks." I could see the guilt practically sweating onto his skin as he stared at a sorrowful Constance.

I knew H was right. I needed to steer clear.

"You have that auction to go to with Izzy on Monday," Dannie said. "That'll take your mind off it."

CHAPTER 17

I walked along the prom towards the cafe, with Constance in my tote bag, having had Sunday lunch at Carol's. I wasn't leaving my cat anywhere. Carol had fussed over her while Rachael kindly spent time with me going over everything for my interrogation with Brad. She'd already contacted the police station and asked for more time and was hopeful that we could put it off, at least a few more days. H hadn't been there; he said he was going to speak to Tara about Constance's abduction.

As I reached home, Lynn met me at the open café doors. "Just in time, lovey," she said. "You've got a visitor." She glanced over at Tara.

Tara smiled at me as I approached. "Can we have a private word?" she said.

Once seated in the snug, Constance settled herself into her bed.

Tara took a deep breath. "Firstly, I can confirm that

the cat-napping was nothing to do with me, or my family. Yes, my brother is not a regular nice guy, but he has three cats himself and would never harm one. In fact he treats his pets a lot better than people. He's even talked about how beautiful your cat is, having seen a picture of her in the newspaper."

Constance gave a small meow from her bed.

"Okay." Although I didn't trust the woman, it felt like the truth.

"As far as Eddie Fly is concerned, I never liked the guy and my brother hated him. He was forever winding Connor up. I try my best to keep my brother in check and people who go out of their way to annoy him get my back up. To be honest, if Eddie had carried on like that, maybe Connor would have dealt with him. But in this instance, he didn't. Honestly, Eddie would never have opened a casino. It takes years to set up and you have to be on the side of the right people, or should I say the wrong people. Eddie Fly was small fry. Connor didn't kill him and," she paused. "If he'd arranged for him to be disposed of, no-one would have found the body."

I shuddered. "I see."

"And now to H."

I blushed feeling a little more than uncomfortable. Was she just about to warn me off her man?

"Yeah, he's good-looking and who wouldn't want to spend time with him? But there isn't much between us other than the odd peck and holding hands. Nothing happened."

"Why's that?" I asked.

"Mainly because he only has eyes for you."

I gulped. "We haven't …"

"You don't have to tell me what you have and haven't done. I know. It's all he talks about."

"Sorry." I knew I'd done nothing wrong, but I didn't know what else to say.

Tara laughed. "No hard feelings. To be honest, the 'dating a policeman' thing was fuelled by my wish to give a powerful message to my brother – to make it clear that I want no part in his dodgy business dealings." She sat back in her seat. "I want to break away from all that. H is great but we have no real chemistry – not like you two."

"So, why are you telling me this?" I asked.

"Because we got off on the wrong foot and I don't want you to think I'm a crazy cat abductor. " She smiled at me. "I want a new life here in Branden Bay. I'm looking at setting up my own gym here. So I don't want anything weird between us."

"Right." I felt a bit of a fool. H had said that Tara was keen to get to know me. And he'd asked me to show her around. Come to think of it, everyone had told me they didn't have a thing going on.

"Do you believe me?" she asked.

I looked into her eyes, she seemed sincere. She glanced over to my murder board, propped in the corner of the snug. I gave a nervous laugh and stood up, inching towards it and then removed her picture before rubbing out Connor's name.

"Ah." She pointed to the board. "Frank's a great chef."

"You know him?" I asked.

She nodded. "He specialises in steaks and French cuisine. He's worked for the casino before." She gave a short laugh. "After seeing him at the casino, Eddie Fly hired him. He was forever copying Connor." She turned to me. "But there was a rumour that Frank had a bit of a thing for Eddie's wife?"

"What, Fiona Fly?" I said, guessing Frank wore a tweed flat cap.

"It was gossip. I don't know her personally."

I took a pen and drew a line between Frank and Fiona on the murder board and turned to Tara. "Tell me, does he like cats?"

"On no." Tara covered her mouth. "H will kill me if you run with that theory."

I laughed. "Come and eat cake with me."

We sat and chatted in the kitchen about the gym Tara was hoping to open. She'd found a unit close to where Jeff worked at the D.I.Y. store. Marcus came in and talked to her about marketing and she oozed excitement about her venture. I felt a pang of jealousy, wishing I could focus just on my business venture instead of life throwing me spirits and ghosts every time things got going.

As I walked her through the café, Lynn approached me. "There's someone else to see you. But don't worry lovey, I've got everything under control."

I looked over her shoulder and spotted the blonde

curly hair. Sitting at a table nursing a cup of tea was Molly O'Brien. She looked up at me, her eyes puffy which I guessed was from crying.

"Hello," she said. "I hope you don't mind me coming to see you. Elena said you were looking into Eddie's murder and now the police seem to think I had something to do with it."

I heard a muffled laugh from Tara. "I'll see you around, Becky." She gave me a small wave as she headed out.

This was clearly the day of awkward chats. I wasn't quite sure if Molly knew it was my fault she had been put on the top of the police's suspect list.

I took her through to the snug. She stared at the murder board. "You think I did it too?"

I shook my head. "I feel strongly that Eddie had feelings for you."

She nodded and dabbed her eyes and sat down on the sofa. Constance woke from her cat bed in the corner and sloped over, I picked her up and put her on my lap as I sat beside Molly.

"So, what's your history?" I asked.

"I met Eddie when I worked the tote at the racecourse. He used to place bets and chat to me. I was so happy when we got together, I thought it was meant to be." She took a breath. "After a year, Eddie started to go quiet on me. I thought he was stressed as he was raising money for his first shop. Then I saw him flirting with Fiona. Now, compared to me, she was proper posh. I blew my top at him and he said let's cool it." She wiped her eyes. "Next thing I know, they got engaged. I was so upset. I left my job."

"Did you ever see him again?"

"Not until Corelli's. I've come out of a long-term relationship and wanted to buy my own place. I'm just about to close on a flat here in Branden Bay, so I got myself a job here and I've been commuting from Bristol until the sale goes through."

"So what did you think when you saw Eddie?"

"As soon as I set eyes on him, I was transported back ten years. But he just blanked me."

"Elena told me she let you go home early."

She nodded. "By the time I reached the bus stop, a text came through from Eddie, saying sorry." She sniffed and pulled out her phone, looking at the text. "He said I was a light shining back into his life. He told me Fiona was going back to Bristol, and that once she'd left, he'd text me." She flashed me the screen showing me the messages. "I showed them to the police and they said they did not have a record of these texts on his phone."

I thought back to my vision, Eddie had a mobile phone on the side of the bath. "So he must have had a second phone." I wondered where that had got to. *Maybe the killer took it?* I thought. But now the police knew the number, they would no doubt be requesting the records from the phone company.

"Eddie asked me to go to his room at Millar's for a chat." She looked back at her phone. "He said his life had been nothing without me in it and was getting a divorce." She burst into tears.

I pulled a tissue from a box on the coffee table and passed it to her. "And then what happened?"

"I went into the Branden Arms to shelter. They called last orders, and I sat sipping my drink when finally, he texted me to say Fiona had gone. He said he'd left the room door on the latch while he freshened up."

"So you met him?"

She shook her head. "I went up to the hotel and Fiona got out of a cab in front of me and went back inside, so I stepped into a shop doorway and texted Eddie, but he never replied."

"Did you see anyone else?"

"Yes. A few people, a couple walking up to the hotel, a man wearing a raincoat pulled over his head and then that guy you were with, in the restaurant, came rushing out." She looked at the door. "I hear he's staying here?" She pursed her lips.

I touched her arm. "Honestly, Marcus is innocent. He saw Eddie had died and thought he might be next if he didn't get away quick. He regrets running now though because, like you say, everyone thinks he did it." I pulled my hand away. "What happened next?"

"An ambulance, police cars and a car showed up. Fiona never came out and Eddie never texted back, by which time I'd missed my bus, so I booked myself a room at the Budget Inn. The next day, I woke up to find out that Eddie was dead." She dabbed her eyes.

"Have you told the police this?"

"I have now. They called me in because the knife turned up at The Budget Inn and they found out I'd stayed there."

I didn't confess that it was me that gave them that piece of information. "It would be helpful if you could tell me a bit about Eddie's background. I heard he was sleeping rough in Bristol until he was taken in by a vicar. How did Eddie come to be on the streets in the first place?"

"He was brought up in a children's home. He didn't like to talk about it. But he told me once, when he was drunk, that it had burned down."

A picture of Eddie's leg came to mind. "Is that how he got that scar on his shin?"

She shrugged. "I guess so. Whenever I mentioned his leg, he said God had punished him. He went to church every Sunday, without fail."

"Was it the church of the vicar that took him in?"

She shrugged. "I don't know."

"Is there anything else you think might be relevant?"

"He used to cry out in his sleep about someone called Dawn, asking her to help him. I didn't know a Dawn, but he woke up crying every time. When I asked him about it, he said it was just a recurring nightmare he'd had since childhood."

I thanked Molly for her help, feeling I was inching closer to the real killer.

CHAPTER 18

*I*t was Sunday evening and I'd called the whole gang over to go through the case. We were about to start our meeting when there was a knock at the cafe door. It was H and I let him in.

"I'm on my way back to Devon. I called in for our chat." He nodded towards my guests. "I didn't realise everyone else would be here." He followed me into the room where the murder board was set up. He shook his head. "Right, let me see what you've got. I might as well know what you're up to, seeing as you won't drop it."

I pointed at the board. "Tara and Conner are no longer suspects."

"Glad to hear it," H said.

"And neither is Molly. I'm trying to build up a picture of Eddie. I've found out that he was brought up in a children's home, which was burned to the ground. Molly confirmed that a vicar and his wife took

Eddie in, and that he used to go to church every week."

"What caused the fire?" Izzy asked.

"I don't know, or where it was situated. Eddie never talked about it. Molly picked up snippets from drunken moments and of him talking in his sleep. He'd call out to someone called Dawn. He has a burn scar on his leg which he says was punishment from God. So I'm thinking that maybe the fire was his fault."

"What else have you got?" H asked.

"Fiona and Frank." I pointed to the line linking their names. "Eddie asked Fiona for a divorce. Rumour has it, she was having an affair with Frank." I didn't mention that Tara had told me. "And I caught Fiona smiling and waving at Frank through the kitchen window at Corelli's. At the time, she pretended she was checking out the cleanliness of the kitchen. I think he also wears a flat cap, and I saw a man in a flat cap coming out of her apartment building and also with her on the Victorian Town Theme Day, not long before my little angel was catnapped."

Constance gave a low meow from her cat bed.

Marcus gave her a quick glance, she'd not gone for him since her dice with death, but he was still wary of her.

"So, his wife had a lover who would have access to knives at Corelli's. That sounds plausible," Lynn said.

"And Eddie said he'd got a meeting with Frank because he owed him money," I added. "So he could have been meeting him the following day also."

"You're so good at this, darling," Izzy said as she made notes.

Dannie shook her head as she typed away.

"Then there's Councillor Nigel Levison," I said. "He's obsessed with his career. It's likely that Eddie had something on him. He clearly said he was meeting him to discuss something the following day."

"He was at the Victorian Town Theme Day as well and could have swiped Constance," Jeff said.

"And what about his wife?" Annie asked.

"Gina Levison was meeting Eddie as well, about what we do not know. I'm keen to speak to her away from her husband. Maybe again there's a scandal Eddie was aware of and they wanted to silence him, considering their imminent elevation to mayor and mayoress."

"You seem to be narrowing it down," H said. "I'm off now. Promise me, Becky, don't go anywhere on your own. And keep that cat locked away."

"Jeff has bought her a GPS collar, so if she goes missing again, I can easily trace her. We're fixing it to her later."

Constance gave a meow of protest.

"I've not been able to get the collar on her yet, it's probably too drab for her." I laughed. "I'll see you out." I followed H to the door, I had an overwhelming urge to grab hold of him for a hug.

He turned and smiled at me. "I mean it. Take care." He gave me a swift peck on the cheek and was gone.

I smiled to myself as I walked back into the café.

THE FOLLOWING MORNING, I waited for Izzy to pick me up and stifled a yawn. I was feeling stiff, having spent another night on the sofa in the snug. Jeff had offered to drive us to the auction rooms, but Izzy had insisted we hired a chauffeur. I wanted to go in the van as I had Constance with me, and she could have stayed in the van with Jeff. We'd managed to pin her down to get the collar on her. She'd scratched away at it, attempting to pull it off but had soon given up. She poked her head out of my tote bag as her fur ruffled in the sea breeze. It was too soon for me to leave her, even though she was wearing a collar. I watched the sea lapping the shore and people were already dotted on the beach with their parasols set up. Breathing in the fresh air, I filled my lungs with the warm air.

A stretch limousine rolled up. "Surely not," I said.

Izzy rolled down the window. "Sweetie."

I laughed. "No worries," I called to the driver as he got out. "I can get in the car myself." I pulled open the door. The inside was luxurious and, once I'd seated myself opposite Izzy, she passed me a glass of fizz.

"What on earth is this for? We're only going to an auction."

Constance jumped from the bag and trotted over to Izzy sitting beside her on the cream leather seat.

"Darling, it's a day out. And I thought you might want a touch of fizz, as it'll be emotional."

"Just one." I smiled at her; it wasn't long past

breakfast.

She stroked Constance's head. "I hope you'll keep your kitty under control today."

My cat meowed loudly, and we both laughed. Izzy was always a great tonic.

Twenty minutes later, we rolled up at the auction rooms.

"We'll be about an hour or so," Izzy said to the driver.

"That's fine, Miss Fallows. I'll be listening to the cricket on the radio." He got out and opened the doors for us.

We walked in and queued for registration. I pushed Constance's head down, into my bag. We registered our interest and were given numbered paddles to use for our bids, I quite fancied the music box I'd seen when I had delivered my furniture.

The room was bustling and the only seats left were to the front, where we seated ourselves on antique pine chairs. I held my bag on my lap with a firm hand on Constance's new collar.

My lots were near to the start, and we watched as one by one my grandma's possessions went under the hammer. I kept having to shush Constance, as she hissed each time the gavel went down. Izzy was right. I felt oddly emotional about it, but I hid my glistening eyes behind tinted glasses and stroked Constance to calm us both down.

"And now we have a brooch."

Izzy looked down at the brochure. She wasn't keen

on fussy jewellery.

"Can I start at five hundred?" Adrian called, looking around the room as silence fell. I realised it was the brooch he'd shown Jeff and me when we visited.

I saw movement to my left and looked over. It was Nigel Levison, rubbing his hands together.

"Izzy," I whispered. "Nigel Levison is here." I looked back at the brooch, realising it must have been him shouting at Adrian about the valuation, when I'd brought my furniture in.

"Where?" Izzy asked.

"Over there." I pointed my paddle at him.

"Thank you, madam," Adrian said, pointing his gavel at me.

Izzy laughed. "Keep that thing down, darling, otherwise you'll be taking that garish thing home with you."

"Five hundred and fifty, anywhere?" Adrian scanned the room with his eyes.

There was silence. My heartbeat quickened. No-one else seemed remotely interested in bidding for it.

"Oh no," I whispered to Izzy.

"Going once at five hundred." He paused with the gavel raised.

"Sweetie, you're stuffed," Izzy said with a laugh.

"Going twice."

The room remained silent.

"Sold to you, madam." He pointed at me as he brought the gavel down with a bang.

Constance wailed from my bag. I'd swapped some pretty decent furniture for an ugly brooch. I turned to check out Councillor Levison. His face was red and lips pursed.

He stormed down the front and barked at Adrian. "Add it to my account."

Constance hissed and struggled to get out of the bag as he left the auction rooms.

I grabbed on to her and turned to Izzy. "Let's follow."

"He's probably going home, sweetie." She looked back at the array of objects up for sale. "I've my eye on a darling art déco figurine."

"Come on, we'll lose him." I stood up.

Izzy rose and looked back wistfully at the auctioneer.

As we reached the exit, we stopped. Levison was on the phone a few paces ahead of us.

"I only got five hundred for it. We can't go on like this, Gina. You need to get a grip. This must stop. Move on and leave that place." He paused while his wife was no doubt speaking. "You're out of control. I'm coming over." He ended the call and swore underneath his breath.

I turned to Izzy and raised my eyebrows.

"See, he's going home," Izzy said. "Let's get back inside."

"He didn't say that, though. She's not at home by the sounds of it. We need to follow."

As Levison marched to his car, Izzy called the

chauffeur over. He swept up in the limo and we opened the doors and got in, just as Levison's Volvo spat gravel as he left the car park.

I leaned forward. "Follow that car."

"Really?" Izzy said. "He's going to notice a stretch limo following."

"I'll be discreet," the chauffeur said. And he was. He held back as far as possible.

"Looks like he's going back to Branden Bay. Just as I thought," Izzy said, but Levison soon turned off the main road.

The driver slowed the limo. "I don't want to get too close."

"What's down here?" I asked, just as I saw the sign to "Hedgebury Retreat."

"It's the spa," Izzy said. "I've been here a few times. It's in a huge old house. It was empty for ages before they restored it."

"So this is where Gina has been," I said.

After waiting a few moments, the chauffeur drove down the lane. As we rounded the bend, we saw a massive Victorian mansion.

"There was a fire here years ago," The driver said. "It used to be a children's home."

I looked at Izzy and gulped.

Her mouth dropped. "Didn't you say Eddie left a children's home after a fire?"

I nodded.

"Coincidence?"

I shook my head. "We're going in."

CHAPTER 19

*W*e walked towards the entrance of the Spa.

"It's difficult to book, but leave it with me, sweetie. I'm sure they can squeeze us in. Just hide your kitty."

I looked down at my bag. Constance was well-hidden, I'd draped a scarf over her head. "There must be some connection between Eddie, Gina and this place," I said. "I can feel it in here." I touched my chest.

As we entered the hall, the receptionist looked up. "Isabella Fallows, what a pleasure." She smiled. "But we have no booking." She looked flustered as she consulted her computer screen. "I'm sorry, there must have been a mix-up."

"No mix-up at all. We were just passing and thought how lovely it would be if you had a room available."

"Our friend is staying here," I added. "We're hoping to meet up with Gina Levison."

"Her husband has just gone up. Would you like me to buzz her room?"

"No need for that," I said hastily feeling Constance wriggling in my bag.

"We do have one twin room left, if you would like me to book you in?" the receptionist asked.

"Yes please," Izzy said.

"Will you be having any treatments?"

"Absolutely," Izzy said. "And we need to visit your boutique as we popped in on the off chance and haven't come prepared."

I could see my reward money evaporating as I looked around the plush reception with wood panelled walls and plush furnishings. The receptionist gave an eye-watering price for the one-night package for two.

I squeezed my hand into my bag. Gliding it around Constance, I fumbled for my credit card holder.

Izzy placed a hand on my arm and handed over her card.

As the receptionist took payment, I whispered to Izzy, "If Gina Levison has been staying here on a long-term basis, no wonder her husband is selling off the family jewels."

Izzy touched my arm. "You'll love this place, darling." She raised one elegant eyebrow at my bag as Constance looked up at us.

I pushed her back down. "I hope I don't love it too much at these prices."

Izzy laughed. "It's my treat."

"No way."

"You're insisting on passing me a share of your reward money. I've already decided I'm going to spend it all on you." She continued. "I've more money than I could ever need. Well, unless I decided I wanted a yacht or something. And I certainly don't want children."

I looked at her waif-like figure. She'd probably look good pregnant and be one of those mothers sporting a tight, cute bump. Whereas I'd probably look more like a space-hopper. "Okay, I'll accept this gift today," I said. "But that's enough."

She gestured towards the door and pulled my arm. "I can't wait to show you around. You'll love it."

Our first stop was the bistro, inside a vast atrium. I gasped. "I thought Millar's was posh." This place was off the scale. And no fake plants here. I could smell they were real and this was confirmed by a member of staff watering them.

"And through here is the spa reception desk where we register for treatments." She gestured down a corridor. "Follow me." The room opened out to a large, tiled, oval space with named treatment rooms. In the space were beds with cosy blankets available, some of which were taken by people reading books and magazines. Izzy opened one of the doors, and we were hit by the smell of eucalyptus and lemon. "The steam rooms and spa."

Constance scrabbled about in the bag, clearly not loving the citrus aromas.

Izzy gestured. "Let's go to the boutique."

"It's an amazing building," I said to the assistant once we were inside the small shop.

"There's been a property on this site since the Victorian times, but sadly it was burned to the ground in the 1990s, leaving only the stone walls. It lay empty for years out of respect, as lives were lost. The owners totally rebuilt it in 2013 when they created the spa."

My body tingled. "So, who died?"

"A couple of kids and a teacher. There are memorials in the garden."

Spasms of static were jumping up and down my body.

"Now, we have a wide selection of swimwear in all sizes." She gestured towards the changing rooms. "Robes, towels and slippers are complimentary, and Chloe will book your treatments at the desk."

Izzy whispered to me as we looked through the rail of swimwear. "What do you think?"

"We need to take a look at the memorial and then see if we can speak to Gina."

We went back to the reception.

"Your room is ready," the receptionist said.

"Thank you," I replied. "We're just going for a stroll around the gardens." I took the key from her. I needed to make sure Constance could have a toilet break because I was going to have to lock her in our room.

Once outside we walked around the gardens, which were beautifully manicured and bursting with colour and fragrance from the plants and flowers.

Izzy pointed to a statue of a nun and two children. "There it is."

We reached the memorial. "In loving memory of Billy, Dawn and Sister Antoinette Gabriel." I read out. I put a hand to my mouth. I gulped. "Dawn? That was the name Molly told me, Eddie had called out in his sleep. What if Eddie had burned the place down."

"And killed not only two children but a nun also?" Izzy said.

"Maybe that's what made him say his scar was a punishment from God," I said.

"You're so close to the truth now, darling. I'm sure Gina must know something."

"The sooner I speak to her the better," I said.

Izzy looked back at the house. "Let's enjoy the facilities and clear your mind. Before planning how to approach this. Then you can interview Gina Levison."

Back in the room, I poured out a shallow glass with water for Constance and told her she'd have to behave, as I could not take her in the spa. She seemed happy to snuggle herself on the bed and I put the do-not-disturb sign on the door. I didn't want her to be discovered by housekeeping.

Downstairs, we made our way to the treatment reception desk. The robes were the same size. On Izzy, it was perfect, showing her delicate calves. She could have wrapped the belt twice around her tiny waist, but on me it was near dragging on the ground. As we reached the desk, I stopped, recognising the voice of the woman in front of me.

"I need to wind down after losing my husband," Fiona Fly said.

Izzy nudged me, as if I hadn't seen her.

Fiona turned around and took a step back in surprise. "Becky." She looked at Izzy. "And Isabella Fallows."

Fiona looked down her nose at my robe. "Sometimes one size doesn't fit all."

"It's a surprise to see you here," I said.

"A surprise, why?"

"Oh, I er ..."

Fiona came over to me and lowered her voice. "Gina invited me. She said she has something she thinks I need to know about Eddie." She sighed. "She's probably going to say he promised a donation and ask me to contribute a huge chunk of his estate. Some people don't even allow you to grieve before trying to get their mitts on your money."

I felt my eye twitch and a buzz of static. Maybe Fiona was in danger?

"I'll no doubt see you around." Fiona walked away with a short wave.

After booking our treatments, we headed for the steam rooms. We sat in the first room.

I breathed in the evocative aromas. "I thought when I moved to the coast, I'd be living a slow-paced life."

Izzy kept her eyes shut as she leaned back. "Darling, you've been reborn."

"Hopefully, when this concludes, I can have a

holiday."

She opened one eye. "Maybe you could go to Devon for a few days."

I laughed. "Have you heard from H today?"

"Darling, he told me to text him every hour to let him know you're still alive."

I sat up. "Why can't he text me himself?"

"I think you know why. Seriously, you need to get out of town and spend an evening with him." She sighed. "Quite frankly, I've been thinking of inviting you both to mine and leaving you to it."

"So, what do you think about Fiona being here?" I said changing the subject.

"Something's afoot for sure."

"I don't like it." I paused. "I'd better check the time, I think my treatment is due."

"I'll see you later, darling."

I decided once we were done, we could collect our thoughts and draw up a plan of action.

Inside the treatment room, I calmed down as the therapist ran her hands through my hair, preparing for my Indian head massage. "I'm going to use essential oils on your scalp. Is that okay with you?"

"Yes," I replied.

"Have you been here before?"

"No, my good friend Gina recommended it, she practically lives here." I thought I would take the opportunity to bring the subject of Gina into the conversation.

"A dear lady. And having to overcome such heartbreak."

"Yes," I said. I wanted to make out I knew what she was on about. "It takes a lot of getting over."

"I know." She lowered her voice, which turned into gossip mode. "Grieving takes years, especially for a brother."

Brother? I thought.

"Are you okay?" she asked. "You jumped. Did I pull a hair?"

"No. Not at all," I said, but I was shocked at the revelation.

When my treatment ended, I found Izzy holding court in the jacuzzi with a couple of older women who were laughing as she spoke. She lifted a glass of fizz. I didn't know how she'd managed to get herself a drink.

"Izzy was telling us about her adventures," said one of the women who wore a turban.

"On the catwalk?" I asked.

"No darling, that's old hat now," Izzy said.

"About your cases, in Branden Bay," said the other woman, who had sleek blonde hair.

"You're not here snooping are you?" giggled the woman with the turban.

I looked to the loungers, feeling eyes upon me. "No, of course not," I said. My voice caught in my throat as Gina peered at me over a book. She was on her own and I guessed her husband had already left after what I imagined was a heated argument. She had clearly decided to stay. To the right of the room, was Fiona and beside her ... *Oh no.* A shaven-haired Frank DuPont was reading a newspaper. Fiona clearly thought a couple of weeks was long enough before parading her new man around. I turned back to the women as I slipped off my robe. "I sold some antiques earlier, at Hedgebury Auction rooms. So we're having a celebratory break on the proceeds."

"I hope you made a lot, because this place is very expensive," the blonde woman added.

I laughed as I entered the water. The jacuzzi bubbles began as soon as I got in and someone called from behind.

"Isabella." It was Chloe, the receptionist. She waved at Izzy.

"My therapist is ready," Izzy said to me. "I'll meet you back at our room later."

Izzy got out of the water like a swan in her white swimsuit carrying her glass of champagne like she was in an advert.

The bubbles fizzed to a gentle flow.

"This place has such a calming feel to it," said the blonde women.

"Yes," I said, feeling incredibly tense.

"We'd better get out. We're going for a wander," the woman with the turban called out over the bubbles.

As they exited the jacuzzi, Fiona and Frank also left. Leaving only myself and Gina. She put her book down, removed her glasses and robe and walked towards the jacuzzi.

She entered the water. "Are you really investigating this place?"

I shook my head vigorously. "No." I gulped. Could Gina's brother have been the boy Billy who died in the fire? My body tingled and I was pretty sure I was close to Eddie's killer. I gulped as tingles shot through my body.

Gina, smiled. She looked younger close-up. Much younger than her husband. A flash of light caught my eye, I turned to the corner of the room and saw a nun standing there. I frowned as the static shot up my neck. It was painful, maybe because I was sitting in water. *She must be warm*, I thought, because the nun was wearing full robes.

"Are you okay?" Gina asked.

"Yes," I said.

I watched the nun put a finger up to her lips.

Gina followed my gaze and the nun fizzled out.

Oh, no! I thought as the static danced around my head. *She was a spirit.*

"Tell me. Do you think honesty is the best policy?" Gina asked.

"Yes," I said, hoping Gina was going to impart some truth in my direction. I needed to know what happened here.

"Do you believe in forgiveness?"

"Definitely," I said.

"There's something I need to get off my chest. A story to be told. Can you meet me in my room later?"

"Of course," I said. "What time?"

"In half an hour. It's a delicate affair." She stared into my eyes. "Don't bring Isabella. I'm in room twenty-three. It's on the top floor."

My mind whirred. *Did Eddie burn the children's home down and kill Gina's brother? Did she kill Eddie as a payback?*

Gina smiled. "I'll see you up there." She got out of the water and as she did, I saw a burn scar up the back of her leg.

CHAPTER 20

*B*ack in my room, my body tingled as I dressed after a quick shower. Constance wailed and I found it difficult to quieten her down.

"Shh, Connie cat. If they find you here, they'll throw us out and we won't find out who killed Eddie."

Constance growled at me.

"Okay, I'll take you with me," I said. I was afraid that if I left her in the room, she'd tear up the carpets at the door. I let out a long sigh. I felt as if I was walking into a trap. *Could Gina have been the one to steal Constance and stuff her in a bag?* She'd been at the Victorian Town Theme Day. I knew from previous cases that looks can be deceiving and while Gina appeared to be a kind lady, she could have a solid heart, especially if it was hardened by the need for revenge. Was her real motive to stop me from discovering the truth?

I checked the time on my phone. Izzy was unlikely to be free to discuss it with me before I met Gina. I stared at the screen. Maybe I should call someone? I instantly thought of H, but there was no point, he was over an hour away and what if I was wrong? I'd already sent the police to Molly, they were unlikely to listen to me again.

I stared at my reflection. "You can do this," I told myself as I slipped my mobile phone into my tote bag before lifting Constance in. I intended to record our conversation. My hands filled with static. *Oh, no,* I thought. I smelled the feint waft of smoke. I opened the guest room door and stepped into the corridor. If it was actual smoke, I knew the fire alarms would be sounding.

Constance gave a low meow from the bag.

I knew this smoke was spirit created. The nun soon appeared in front of me, beckoning, frantically. My instinct was telling me that this was Sister Antoinette Gabriel.

You can do this, I told myself as I followed her down the corridor and up the stairs. When we reached the next floor, she pointed ahead. The buzzing sensation intensified up my back and hot static filled my arms.

"This way," I heard her whisper. As I turned the corner, I saw Fiona standing at a door with twenty-three written on it. The nun ignored Fiona and walked through the door without opening it.

Fiona shuddered and rubbed her arms as if she'd felt a breeze. "Have you come to see Gina?" she asked me.

I heard a scream in my head, like wind charging

through my ears. It took my breath away. I nodded at Fiona. Taking a deep breath, I stared at the closed door and felt quite faint. I leaned on the wall to steady myself and felt Constance wriggle in the bag.

The ghostly nun whooshed out. "She was pushed," she cried, and then sped down the stairs.

"Oh my goodness," I said and moved toward the door as Fiona stepped aside. I knocked on the door. "Mrs Levison? Gina?"

"She's not answering," said Fiona, "I already knocked twice I was just about to leave when you got here."

"Have you tried the door?"

"Of course not."

I heard another cry, but this time, it wasn't a ghostly one. It was someone calling for help outside.

"Gina? It's Becky. Are you okay?" I tried the handle, and found the door was unlocked. I gingerly pushed it open and went inside.

Fiona followed behind. "Gina, are you okay?" she asked.

There was a neatly-made bed, but no sign of Mrs Levison.

"She's not here," Fiona said looking around the room.

I heard voices shouting from the open window as the curtains billowed inwards. I placed my bag with Constance in it, on the bed and walked onto a stone balcony which ran all the way along the upper floor. I peered over the edge to the lawns below. Two people were standing over a person on the floor and looked up at me. Slumped between them was Gina. Her body lay like a discarded rag doll.

"No!" Fiona shouted from my side and put her hand to her mouth. "She jumped."

"Or someone pushed her," I said, crossing my arms. Had Fiona pushed her over the edge and then exited the room just as I came up the stairs? I looked along the balcony, realising that anyone who pushed her could have easily escaped. I returned to the bedroom. On the dressing table was a large envelope. It had *Sorry* written on it in large, scrawled letters.

Nigel Levison entered the room with a huge case in his hand. "What are you two doing in here?" he demanded. "Where's my wife? I've come to collect her." He looked at me, Fiona, and then at the envelope. He approached the desk and stared at it. His hands shook as he picked it up.

I gasped as cutlery fell from the envelope to the floor. I recognised it from Corelli's.

"I guess that's her confession," Fiona said as she put a hand to her chest and slumped onto the bed. "I can't believe it. So Gina killed my Eddie?" She looked up at Nigel. "I said, your wife killed my husband."

"I'll ask again," Levison said. "Where is my wife?"

The manager entered the room. "Will you please come with me downstairs?" Her face was ashen.

Levison pushed past me to the window.

"Don't," I said but he continued to the balcony.

"Gina," he shouted as he looked to the ground below. "What has she done?"

I felt rooted to the spot, panting, catching my breath as the static dissipated.

Constance, who was now out of the bag on the bed, wailed. I shot an apologetic glance to the manager.

"No," Levison shouted, before turning around. "She's killed herself?"

Someone shouted up to us. "She's still breathing."

I puffed out in relief. As much as Gina was likely to be Eddie's killer. It would be much simpler if she gave a proper confession. Nigel Levison darted out of the room nearly knocking the manager over.

Fiona put her hand to her forehead. "Why?"

I sat next to her. "Hopefully we'll find out." I didn't want to explain about the fire. That her husband Eddie had lived in the house as a child. That he had likely set the place alight and killed three people, including a boy called Billy who may have been Gina's brother. It wasn't my place and I wondered whether Fiona had really ever cared about her husband, especially as she was now parading her new chef boyfriend around. And even though Gina had left a confession of sorts with evidence, something didn't feel right to me. There were huge pieces missing from this puzzle.

As I followed Fiona and the manager out of the room, I knew for sure that something was afoot because I heard the ghostly nun's voice again in my head. *She was pushed.* Whether or not Gina was guilty of Eddie's demise, someone else had just tried to end her life. A killer was still at large.

I WOKE the next morning with my alarm at six. I'd spent the best part of the night at Branden Bay police station giving a full statement to D.C.I. Brad Harris. I thought he may have let me off the interview about stealing personal data, but no, he'd merely postponed it to another day. He seemed convinced that Gina had killed Eddie, considering the collection of steak knives found in her room and the apparent link between her, Eddie, and the children's home. The police would no doubt be doing background checks. But they would not be able to interview Gina, as she was in a coma. Annoyingly, Brad wouldn't let Marcus leave town either, until he had Gina's full confession.

After a busy morning, I sat with Lynn.

"I'm pleased to see your gift is developing," she said. "Seeing the nun at the spa. What a sad story for Gina Levison? Grief can eat away at people, especially if there's someone to blame."

"We won't know the full story unless she wakes up." I shook my head. "I don't know how you cope with it. Connecting to dead people all the time. Taking on their pain."

She sat back. "Us mediums are sensitive by nature. That's why we can pick up the emotions left behind in the physical world in the first place. And we can also connect to people still alive." She looked at a couple sitting nearby. "I can sense what they're feeling. Can you?"

I nodded. "The guy is upset about something." I looked away, not wanting to take on any more negative emotions.

"Now tell me about this nun, Sister Antoinette Gabriel," Lynn said.

"She led me to Gina. Then she rushed out and said that Gina was pushed." I stood up. "I can't just sit here. I know Gina didn't jump off that balcony. I can feel it in here." I placed a hand on my chest. "I need to get to the hospital."

"Hey, lovey, sit down. You need to rest."

But I ran up to Jeff's room and asked him to drive me over to the hospital. He was due in work in an hour but said he would take me.

I JUMPED out of the van at the hospital, leaving Constance with Jeff. I was pretty sure taking animals onto a ward was against the rules.

Once inside, I saw Nigel Levison, buying a cup of tea at the refreshments kiosk.

"How is she?" I asked as I approached him.

"She's not woken yet," he sighed. "They doubt she'll make it. And if she does, she could be in a vegetative state."

"Oh no. That's awful."

He nodded. "She's under a non-resuscitation order

so they have turned off the ventilator. It'll be up to her to pull through, if she really wants to live."

"But she must only be early forties? Does she have any family that can come and help? Any brothers and sisters who can look after her?"

"No. She has no relatives that she is in contact with. And she always said to me that she'd rather be dead than dependant. And the police will grill her. I don't want her to suffer like that. She wanted to end her life and I respect that. What sort of life is she going to have? She'll see the rest of her days in prison." He took a deep breath. "She's my wife, and I respect her wishes."

"Can I see her?"

He frowned. "What for?"

"I've had a shock, seeing her on the ground like that. I need it for closure."

He nodded. "Okay, I'll take you." He led the way.

I reached the I.C.U., and Gina lay on the bed in traction, with a bandage around her head. I sat down and held her hand. A nurse came in and called Nigel Levison away.

I stroked Gina's hand and shut my eyes, trying to connect with her. I felt with all my heart that she had been pushed and regardless of whether or not she'd killed Eddie, no-one should take her life. *Are you in there, Gina?* I said in my head, trying to connect to her spirit. I heard her stir. Her voice rasping. I snapped open my eyes, to see her struggling to open hers.

Her mouth moved. "He killed my brother," she said in a rasping voice.

"I know, Gina. I know." I presumed she was talking about Eddie killing her brother Billy, having set the home alight.

"Did you kill Eddie?" I asked.

She moved her head. "No. My brother. He's my brother. Was."

I sat blinking for a while, digesting what she had said. "Did you say Eddie was your brother?"

"Yes. We were only children. Accident. He wants me dead. Help." She drifted off.

"Gina, Gina." I squeezed her hand as alarms sounded on the monitors.

A nurse came in. "Did she wake?"

I turned around. "Yes. She said 'help', she does not want to die."

"Are you sure?"

I stood up. "Definitely."

Nigel Levison came in. "What's going on?"

The nurse checked the printouts and he called the doctor in. "The records show significant brain activity. And Mrs Levison spoke to this lady."

Nigel frowned at me. "What did she say?" he demanded. He seemed upset. I guess he was fed up that he'd missed it and was not there to speak to her himself.

"We need to contact the police," the nurse said to Nigel Levison. "They told us to alert them if she came to."

A vein in Nigel's neck moved. I realised how stressful it was for him. I did not want to tell him what I had learned, and needed to get out of there to gather my thoughts.

WHEN I REACHED THE VAN, Constance pawed at the window and I opened the door.

"I have to go straight to work," Jeff said.

"I'm sorry, I forgot the time." I grabbed Constance. "I need to think, anyway. I'll walk back."

I walked around the hospital towards town. There was a peaceful stretch of road which ran alongside the cricket field. It was quiet with no-one about and I took a deep breath and brought a picture up in my mind of my murder board, as Constance trotted at my feet. I mentally drew a line from Gina to Eddie. *They were brother and sister, why does no-one know this?* I asked myself. And Gina had said, 'He killed my brother.' I presume this referred to the person that also pushed her off the balcony. The same person wanted her dead and she had said the fire was an accident. Faces swam in front of my eyes but seeing the murder board in my mind, I knew it could only be one of two people. I stopped in my tracks and reached for my phone. This time I needed to call the police, but as I pulled my phone from my pocket, it vibrated with an incoming call from Dannie.

I answered it, hearing a car driving close to me and

scooped Constance in my arms, I didn't want her straying into the road.

"Becky, where are you?" Dannie asked. "The café is heaving and I've had to ask Marcus to help out front, when you asked me not to."

"That doesn't matter, Dannie. Look, I have something important to tell you about who killed Eddie Fly."

"Who?" Dannie asked. "Shall I call the police? Where are you?"

Someone yanked me from behind, snatching the phone from my hand. I heard it fall on the concrete path. I struggled as they put their big hand tight across my mouth and nose. Constance wailed and Gina's voice repeated in my head. *He killed my brother.* And all the pieces floated in front of my eyes, until they fitted together like a jigsaw puzzle. I passed out.

CHAPTER 21

I woke, wondering where I was. It was dark and I felt like I had a hangover. Exhaust fumes filled my nostrils and I heard a loud car engine. As I became more awake, I felt the motion of being driven, but I wasn't in a car seat. No, I was in the boot. I heard a long meow. *Yes.* I reached out to find Constance and fumbled around her neck. She was still wearing the GPS collar. Memories of what had happened seeped into my mind, I just hoped Dannie realised someone had abducted me and asked Jeff to trace us. *Oh, please.* I realised the person driving us was likely to have killed Eddie and pushed Gina off the balcony. There was no way they were going to spare my life.

I fumbled around the boot to see if my phone was there. I couldn't locate it but my hand rested on rough material. Maybe it was tweed. *Oh, a tweed cap.* I flushed hot. I was as good as dead and knew that as soon as they lifted the boot, I was going to have to fight for my life. I spent the time focussing on my reasons to live: To see my parents again. To continue making people smile when they came to the café. To provide a home for my strays, Constance, Dannie and Jeff. To maybe have a romance with H. To be a best friend to Annie and Izzy and a support for Lynn. With every thought of those I love, I become stronger. I wasn't going to be the next victim.

It seemed like we were driving forever. I pulled my cat towards me. "Constance, I will not let him kill us."

The car left the smooth road and was banging about, up and down, as if we were driving across rough terrain. My head hit the lid of the boot and a can of de-icer flung around, hitting me in the face. That made me mad, really mad. I breathed in deeply, and fumbled around for the de-icer, this guy was going to get a surprise when he lifted the lid. I held onto Constance, wondering where on earth we were going until we came to an abrupt halt. I placed Constance beside me, knowing she would also be going in for the kill.

As soon as light peeled in, I kicked the boot with all my strength, then sprayed the de-icer.

"Ouch! My chin."

I frowned. It wasn't the voice I was expecting.

"You're alive?" Nigel stood with his hand to his face, spitting de-icer from his mouth.

Constance dived at him.

"Get off," he screamed, his arms flaying around.

I took advantage of the distraction. I scrambled out of the boot and rushed at him. He took a step backwards then fell over a rock.

"My ankle," he cried out.

Constance jumped from him and we both watched as he writhed around on the floor and proceeded to sob. I took some much-needed deep breaths as I stared at him clutching his injury. I couldn't believe this guy was a killer and a wife-killer too? Just about as evil as you could get.

Nigel looked up at me. "I thought I'd suffocated you. You slumped to the floor and I couldn't find a pulse."

Failed murder attempts seem to be his style, I thought, as I looked at his twisted foot. There was no way he was going to be able to overpower me, it looked broken. "Why, Nigel? Why? I don't understand?"

"You're an interfering, busybody. Sticking your nose into other people's business." He paused to cry out in pain as he attempted to move. "I just wanted to stop you interfering. I didn't mean to hurt you, I just lost it." He continued with his sobbing.

"I meant why did you kill Eddie Fly?" I asked.

He shook his head. "I never killed the man, Gina did."

Constance hissed and I stroked her to calm her down.

Levison's eyes were wild as he looked up at me. "All

our dreams of being mayor and mayoress are shattered. I've no idea what that man did to her, to drive her to something so heinous, to stab the man in the neck." Nigel shuddered. "He must have been evil to the core. My poor Gina. She's the sweetest woman you could ever meet. Every Sunday, she goes to church, teaching children about right and wrong. How could she have done it?" he cried.

"Calm down, Nigel."

He wiped his eyes on his sleeve. "Gina and I were truly happy. Now she's killed a man then tried to kill herself. And what am I? A kidnapper? What have I done? My whole world has collapsed. I'm so sorry."

I took a moment to scan where we were, I needed to get hold of his mobile phone and call the police, so I needed our location. I couldn't drive him back, I hadn't learned to drive. As I scanned the place, I saw we were in a field next to a wooded area. The Quantock Hills were in the distance, I recognised them as Grandma used to have a friend who lived nearby. I realised we were in the southern part of Somerset. I saw the tracks across the field, the car had driven down and at the edge, by the road, another car was parked. *That's handy, probably someone walking their dog.* I thought. *At least I can ask them for help.*

"You're under a lot of pressure," I said to Nigel in an attempt to calm him down. "Take a breath. Why do you think Gina killed Eddie? Wasn't she with you that night?"

"We'd argued about her wanting to meet him, so I poured myself a Bourbon and fell asleep in front of the TV. I guess she slipped out. And the note, of course with the knives in her room. And she's not been herself since."

Constance hissed, and I looked around, someone had got out of the car parked on the edge of the field. I squinted at the man approaching, he didn't have a dog with him, although he appeared to be carrying a stick. *Oh, no.* I grabbed Levison's arm. "There's a man with a gun." I tried to pull him up. "Where is your mobile phone?"

"Slow down," he said. "I come to this field to shoot pheasant." He pointed. "Look, he's wearing a hunting cap. I've got one in the boot."

I looked up. Yep, it was a cap alright, and although I couldn't see it up close, I had a feeling it was tweed and that he was indeed a hunter. But the fizzing of static running up my body told me he wasn't here for the pheasants.

"Nigel listen to me. Gina did not kill Eddie. Frank DuPont did and he pushed Gina over the balcony. Nigel, if we don't get out of here, he's going to kill us too," I shouted. "Up."

Nigel squinted. "You mean the chef?"

"Yes."

"Why?"

"I'll explain later. Give me your phone."

"I can't find it," he said putting his hands in his pockets.

"We need to move, fast."

He cried out in pain as he tried to get up.

"Come on." I helped him to standing and looked out over the field. Frank was getting closer and was already within shooting distance. He lifted his gun.

"Lean on me," I said as I heard a helicopter above us, praying it belonged to the police.

I dragged Levison into the trees, finding a strength I didn't know I had. He cried out, as we slowly moved ahead, out of sight and into the wood. But I knew Frank would be gaining on us.

"Over there." Levison pointed "There's a hut. I often use it when I'm out here."

We reached the small wooden shack and I opened the door, and stepped inside. It would be no defence against a gun. I felt like we were the second of the three little pigs, waiting for the wolf to show up. If Frank found us, we were doomed. We lay on the floor in silence. Sirens were carried on the breeze. Relief washed over me, until I heard a French accent.

"They killed my sister. She was a good woman, a bride of Christ."

I stood up.

"Becky, no," Levison whispered.

I knew the only way to delay Frank would be to keep him talking.

I opened the door. "How did you find out that Eddie started the fire?"

"I came to England for the unveiling of the memorial at the Hedgebury Retreat, in memory of my sister. I stayed in Bristol and saw a job advertised in Bristol's casino. I wanted to be close. I was later hired by Eddie Fly, he was drunk after his dinner guests had left. The disgusting man. He asked me why I was running away from France. I said I had no reason to."

"And then he told you he'd run away himself?" I asked. "After causing a fire at a children's home?"

"I knew it must be him that killed Antoinette, but I hired a private detective. Not a stupid amateur like you, someone with connections on the inside. They provided pictures of the children who went missing. A brother and sister called Billy and Dawn. I recognised Eddie from the picture and the investigator discovered that he met Gina at church every week and that she resembled the picture of Dawn."

I heard Nigel mumbling behind me. I realised hearing this must have been a shock to him. Discovering his wife had kept such a big secret from him. But he didn't speak.

"They were only children," I said.

"They had lives; much longer than my sister."

"So you got close to Eddie's wife?"

He laughed. "I did not realise Fiona would be so willing. As if I would be interested in that self-centred woman."

"You used her, to keep tabs on her husband."

"She constantly told me where he was, as she was avoiding him so she could spend time with me."

"And then you struck out of anger?" I listened out for the sirens but I could no longer hear them. How long could I keep him talking? Maybe the police were not coming and Jeff had not been able to track us on the GPS.

"I was planning something cleaner," Frank said. "I hated him. It was messy, too messy. I grabbed knives from Corelli's. He'd humiliated me."

"You knew the layout of Millar's Hotel. I guess you'd worked there at some point?"

"A lucky guess."

"So you avoided the CCTV, going in and out through the staff entrances."

"After I killed him, I heard the lift open, and hid in a doorway, seeing that idiot boyfriend of yours go in, he was easy to frame. When I reached the outside, I saw that Fiona had returned. She nearly spotted me. I ran down the road, got in my car and drove to Bristol. I phoned her later to find out where she was, telling her I was waiting outside her apartment. She would never have thought it was me."

"She won't like it when she finds out you killed Eddie."

"She won't find out. No loose ends, which is why I am here." He gave an evil laugh. "I may even stick around, now Fiona is a rich woman. And thanks to that stupid man in there abducting you while I watched. Now I can kill you both and blame him." He pointed at the shack with his gun.

Over Frank's shoulder, I saw what I'd been waiting for, someone moving stealthily between the trees.

Keep him talking some more, I told myself. "The fire was an accident."

"They ran away, started new lives for themselves. My sister was a beautiful, innocent creature, only twenty-five and put on the earth to help others. And I told Mrs Levison that before I pushed her."

"Your sister wouldn't want you to kill, she was a good person."

"Don't speak about her as if you know her. You never knew her."

I gulped, maybe I'd pushed him too far.

He raised his gun. "You should have kept out of it. I warned you in the note I left with your stinking cat."

I saw a flash of orange whizz by, as Constance dashed out of the shack. Frank turned, following her body with his gun as if he was lining up his prey.

"No," I dived as he turned to the side and I tackled him rugby-style. Nigel screamed as he followed before slumping his body on top of us. We both pinned Frank to the ground, while pellets rained out of his gun as my ears rung. He wriggled underneath us as I gingerly looked up, smelling the gunpowder and checking for my cat.

"Constance?" I called out.

With relief I heard her meow, and it wasn't a pitiful one. Within seconds, there was a swarm of uniformed officers. Once Frank was safely detained, H reached me, and pulled me up then held me so close, I felt his heart thumping as my cheek pressed against his chest. Constance wailed at our feet.

"Detective Sergeant." I heard the recognisable growl of Bad Cop Brad. "Put her down."

H ignored him and did not let me go.

"Get her out of here!" Brad shouted when we didn't move.

H took me by the hand and I picked up Constance and carried her, as he lead us across the grass towards the road where Jeff stood by the van. I glanced back to see Nigel on the floor being attended to by paramedics.

"I told Jeff to wait in his van," H said. "He wanted to come. If it hadn't been for him and that GPS collar on Constance, we'd never have found you." He stopped and turned to me. "When I heard the gun go off, I thought I'd lost you." He looked down at me, picking grass out of my hair. "Why do you never listen?"

"If I hadn't made a fuss, Gina would have been blamed for Eddie's death and Frank would have got away with it."

"Becky," Jeff called.

I tore my eyes away from H and waved at Jeff, who ran up to us.

"You gave us a scare," he said, panting.

I passed Constance to H and hugged Jeff. "Thank you so much. You literally saved our lives."

"After Dannie called, I turned on the GPS and saw Constance was on her way to South Somerset. I called H, and we met just up the road. Then" H called in the number plate on car, which we found out was Frank DuPont's. He frowned as the stretcher passed us. "Why is Councillor Levison here?"

"I was just taking a drive with him," I lied. "When Frank showed up."

"That's a long drive, we thought you'd been abducted. You were cut off when speaking to Dannie. Then we couldn't get hold of you."

"Oh, I must have dropped my phone," I said, giving a nervous laugh as Nigel reached us on a stretcher. I grabbed his hand. "Councillor Levison needs to get to the hospital, to help Gina get better. They've got a whole new life to lead and a town that needs a mayor and mayoress. He's had quite a fright having been followed here by Frank, when we were just out for a drive." I squeezed his hand hoping he had registered what I would be putting into my statement. I let go and he cried as they carried him away. I saw no point in Nigel Levison going to prison for my abduction, Gina had had a tough childhood, lost her brother, and had survived an horrific fall. She needed her husband, as imperfect as he was and he had helped me pin Frank down, which must have hurt, considering his injury. I may have died without him.

H raised his eyebrows at me. "Let's get back to Branden Bay." He took my hand, and I felt pleasant tingles up my arm.

It was some hours before we got back to the house, having had to give a statement to the police which wasn't totally true. Jeff had taken Constance back for me and was asked to give his statement the following day.

"I still want that chat with you," H said as we entered the house.

"It won't be tonight," I replied, when we were greeted by all of our friends.

CHAPTER 22

"It's time," Lynn said.

She'd wanted to make sure that the moving on, of Eddie, AKA Billy, was performed perfectly. He had still been in my bathroom, but the vision had faded. I only felt static and saw a light. We met in the spiritualist hut, because it would have been impossible to get Gina up the stairs at my house in her plaster casts. She'd decided to keep the name Gina and not revert to Dawn, even though the truth was out. Other than Gina, there were only mediums present, and Constance was there too. Jeff was out conducting a ghost hunt up at Branden Bay castle.

I looked around the room at the collection of women and one man. A couple of the mediums appeared to recognise my cat, calling her by name, and had a chat as she meowed away. They looked over at me and gave a knowing smile. Maybe they'd seen

Constance in the café, or read about the psychic cat in the newspaper.

Lynn announced the start of the session.

"Billy, known as Eddie. Come in," Lynn said. "I've got Dawn here, also known as Gina."

Eddie appeared before us, luckily he wasn't naked, indeed he was only a boy, dressed in pyjamas.

"Is he there?" Gina whispered. The bandages had been removed from her head, but her bruising was still present and both legs, plus one of her arms were in casts.

I squeezed her free hand and nodded.

"Billy, lovey, it's time to leave," Lynn said.

A slither of light appeared and grew wider until a young woman stood within the glow.

"I have a June here," Lynn said.

Gina whispered. "It's our mother."

The spirit of June opened her arms and the young Billy ran to her and she embraced him. June turned and looked at Gina then to me. In my head I heard her voice. "Tell Dawn I love her. I'll always be waiting."

I swallowed hard and took a deep breath. "Your mum told me to tell you she loves you and will always be waiting for you."

As soon as I'd said it, they passed in a flash and the room fell silent.

Lynn approached us and comforted Gina in a motherly fashion until she had stopped crying.

"Thank you so much," Gina said to Lynn who released her and then went to sort the refreshments.

Gina turned to me. "I don't want my brother to be forgotten. I've told Isabella, that I'm happy for her to write the full story about the accident at the home."

A lady came around distributing cups of tea and biscuits. We both took some and sipped our teas. I waited for Gina to talk, I didn't want to press her, while she was emotional. After a while she opened up again.

"We didn't mean to set the place alight, and for poor Sister Antoinette Gabriel to die. Eddie was afraid of the dark. We snuck up to the top room one night, with a candle and we fell asleep. We both woke to find the place on fire, we burned our legs running to safety. We were frightened about being told off, so we ran away. Then saw in the newspaper that Sister Antoinette Gabriel had died and the building was totally gutted with the floors collapsing."

"You must have been so scared," I said.

She nodded. "At the time the newspapers concluded that we had been cremated in the blaze. And if they were looking for our remains, they wouldn't have found them as we were not in our designated rooms. They thought we'd died in the fire. And then we sheltered in a church. After confessing to Pastor Mike, he said we deserved a fresh start and believed in new beginnings. He was on witness protection himself, having had a shady past. He helped us set up new identities. They were a childless couple, it worked well for all of us."

"So why did you not tell everyone you were siblings?"

"The children they used for our identities were not related, so we never told anyone we were brother and sister, and just referred to each other as a friend from church. If I had told Nigel I was adopted, he would have urged me to trace my real family. It had the potential of unraveling a past Eddie and I intended to keep secret." She sighed. "Once you tell one lie, you tell another and another. Although Eddie was having difficulty with his success. He said he wanted to release his guilt. He had an urge to face the past which I did not share. He said we were innocent children and would not face charges. But I was reluctant, with Nigel and I being in the local public eye. I wanted to keep our secret."

"Where are the Wrights now?"

"They were an elderly couple when they took us in and died some years ago." She sighed. "Poor Eddie, I was so proud of my brother. And now I want everyone to know that. It's time for the truth."

"He's at peace now, Gina," I said. "I wish you could have seen his spirit, such a happy young lad," I said.

"And Nigel has spoken to the Council, and they said that they judge the mayor and mayoress on their works, not on things that happened in their childhood."

"If you don't mind me asking, what was it you wanted to speak to Eddie about when you saw him in Corelli's?"

She laughed. "The same thing that Nigel wanted to talk to him about. Eddie did have a way of winding

Nigel up and the betting shop did not fit into Branden Bay High Street. He had not been to church for a few weeks and I knew I would not see him before the Council met. I wanted to explain to him exactly why the shop was not right for our town and to ask him to drop it. It was never going to go through, and I didn't want it to turn nasty between him and Nigel. I wanted Eddie to withdraw the application, rather than have it rejected."

"How is Nigel?" I said, as I saw the rest if the party leaving. A couple of them waved at me as they fussed over Constance.

"Fine," Gina said. "I'm pleased to get it out in the open. We've never been so close." She patted my hand. "He told me exactly what happened. You truly have a compassionate heart."

I smiled. I was so relieved that the whole nightmare was over.

CHAPTER 23

A week later, I took my washing out to the garden to dry on a line which Marcus had hooked up for me. Things had calmed down after Izzy's latest story had been published in the Gazette with the headline: *French Assassin Thwarted by Local Heroes*. Both myself and Levison had come out well from it. He was back to his stiff-upper-lip when I saw him. His lower leg was in a cast but he had flashed me a couple of smiles when no-one was looking.

H told me that Brad wasn't convinced by my statement of what happened on the day Frank was caught. But, with no other witnesses, he didn't intend to pursue it and had dropped the charge against me wasting police time, considering the glowing report Izzy had printed.

I'd heard that Fiona had moved in with her parents as news got out that she'd been having an affair with

Frank the murderer, and rumours started that she'd put him up to it. Which of course, wasn't true but I wasn't feeling any sympathy for her.

I pegged a dress on the line. It was such a nice day. Unfortunately for Frank DuPont, he would not be seeing such a sunny day again, because he'd suffered an accident inside prison while on remand. He'd slipped and knocked his head on a hand basin and died.

"God moves in mysterious ways," Lynn had said. H thought there was foul play and mentioned organised crime. As awful as it was, I felt relieved as I seemed to be racking up court cases in which I had to appear as a witness. The first one was in a couple of weeks, and I wasn't looking forward to coming face to face with the killer again.

Marcus called me from the back door. As I approached, he stretched his arms out towards me. I placed my empty basket on the ground, he moved forward and let him embrace me. It was, after all, goodbye.

"How did we get here, Becky?" he said as we hugged on the patio.

"I know," I said, feeling that we now had a friend-ship. Releasing him, I smiled. "I wish you well, Marcus. It seems we've both changed."

"I'm glad we made up," he said. "I've a small favour I'd like to ask."

"A loan?"

"No, I've been offered a contract, actually."

"Oh, great. Is it another firm of accountants?"

He shook his head. "No, I'm done with that. I'm starting a consultancy business. It's helping a start-up, beginning at the ground level."

"Good for you," I said. "What time's your train?"

"Here's the thing ..."

A car hooted in the distance. "That's for me. I'm helping Tara set up her gym. Do you mind if I stay here for a while until I get a place of my own?"

I took a deep breath. I didn't have the energy to argue with him. "Okay. But please, not for too long."

He took my hand and led me through the house to the front door. "Becks, you've saved me from a life behind bars. I won't outstay my welcome."

I watched him walk down the path towards Tara's car.

I glanced at my phone, then stared at my reflection in the porch mirror. Yes, my hair could still do with a cut, but I looked fine. I was expecting H. Finally, we were going to have our chat. No interruptions. The café was closed. I'd told everyone we needed to be alone. I'd even locked Constance in the snug.

Five minutes later, he came into the quiet house.

"Where is everyone?" he asked. "I hear Tara has taken Marcus on."

"I know. He needs to find somewhere else to live. I really don't want my ex living with me."

"I might be able to help you out there," H said. "He can stay at mine."

"On no. Trust me, he's way too annoying. He'd

drive you crazy." I also felt it was weird, my ex living with my new man. If that's what he'd come over to discuss – for us to have a go at it.

"I won't be there," H said.

I frowned.

"A permanent position has come up in a small town outside of Exeter. It's a great opportunity."

"So that was what you wanted to chat to me about?"

He shook his head. "Events have changed. This town isn't big enough for the both of us. I need something to get my teeth into now I'm a detective sergeant. I want to make a difference."

"Sometimes mediums and detectives team up and solve mysteries," I said.

"Yeah," he said with a laugh. "On TV."

I took his hand and felt a buzz through my fingers as I laced them in his. *It's now or never.* I had to show him how I felt. I moved forward and looked up at him. As soon as I reached him, he pulled me close, then lifted me up. I felt his heart beating hard against my chest, as our lips met.

After the sweetest kiss, he lowered me to the ground and moved a hair from my face. His eyes were dark and his pupils were large."You choose your moments," he said. "We could have done this months ago."

I laughed. "Tell me about it."

"But I still have to go." He paused. "You understand, don't you?"

"Long-distance relationships. Do they ever work?" I asked.

"Only time will tell." He smiled at me. "I'll see you next Sunday, I'm back for dinner at Ma's, then we can go on our first proper date, if you want to that is?"

I laughed. "Of course I want to."

He looked at his watch. "I have to get off to Devon now, as I start in two hours."

I watched from my gate as he drove along the prom until he rounded the bend. My heart felt heavy, but the psychic in me knew he'd be back.

AFTER AN HOUR of moping and cuddling Constance, there was a ring at the door. I opened it to find the biggest bouquet I'd ever seen. I looked at the flowers and grinned. *How thoughtful of H.* Although it was over the top and I didn't have him down as a roses type of guy. Especially not this many. *These must have cost a couple of hundred, at least,* I thought. And the crystal vase they came in. *Wow, he must have had a raise with his position.*

"Can you bring them through?" I said as a second woman followed with a box of chocolates which was literally a meter wide and on top of it was a vacuum-packed salmon. I laughed. "He loves you too, Constance."

My cat stared up at me, watching the women walk through the house. I asked them to place the gifts on my kitchen table and one handed me a card as they left.

Dannie came in through the back door. "Wow, someone's popular."

I laughed. She swiped the card from my hand.

"Hey, that's mine. It's private."

She read it to herself. "Oh," she said and spun around. She bit her lip, then sniggered before passing it to me. "Good luck with that one."

I huffed as I took the card and she left the room. I smelled the sweet bouquet of the blooms as Constance growled. I guessed she wanted me to stop faffing about and open the salmon. "Be patient," I said as I turned the card over to read it.

Becky,

Congratulations on solving your latest case.

You are an amazing woman.

The words filled my heart to bursting, as much as H had told me to keep out of police business, he clearly respected my detecting skills.

Do not fear. I have your back, for now and always. You will be kept safe. No-one will do you wrong and get away with it.

"Oh, how sweet," I said aloud.

Constance gave a low meow.

Please let me treat you to dinner.

Yours, if you'll have me.

I was practically grinning from ear to ear, feeling that H clearly was up for a long-distance relationship. Until I read the last line:

With love, Connor Davies xx
"Oh no," I groaned. "That's all I need."

The End

ACKNOWLEDGMENTS

I'd like to thank my creative writing tutor Rosemary Dun, both inside the OU and out! You encouraged me to pursue novel writing and gave me so much information and guidance, I'm still reading the handouts! You are amazing. Thanks also goes to my brilliant mentors Alison Knight and Jenny Kane of Imagine Creative Writing and their Novel in a Year course, which gave me lots of help and kept me on track. And Alison is also my editor - thanks for all you do xx

Thanks to my cover artist Daniela www.stunning-bookcovers.com who is amazing - I spend a lot of time gazing at her website.

Thanks to the inspirational friends I met through the Romantic Novelists' Association, and the Bristol writing community (I'm too scared to list everyone in case I miss someone off!) And to my Beta readers

Cinnomen Matthews McGuigan, Michelle Armitage, Shell Rice Mortimer and Leanne Goodall. Thanks also to Helen Blenkinsop who is a guru on the 'hook' and amazon ads. And thanks to my best writing friends – Callie Hill, Claire O'Conner and Jenny Treasure, for also being beta readers and for sharing the journey with me, especially Callie who is always there to listen.

Thank you to my advance reader team who are really supportive and there for me, even from the first book. And especially Carol Kurimbokus who picks up those last pesky typos. I really appreciate it.

Thank you to those on my mailing list who interact with me. And thanks to those who send me cake ideas: Val, Keith, Carolyn, David, Janice, Tanith, Pamela-Anne, Nancy, Carrie-Ann, Carol, Sylvia, Marion, Christie and Betty. Keep them coming!

Thanks to Tracey Hadfield who always has a ghost hunting story to scare me with.

Thanks to my sassy cats, even though they boss me about on a daily basis.

Thanks to my family for supporting me and reading my books, especially Dad, Uncle Stephen and Debjita.

And finally, thanks to Gary for putting up with me tapping away at the keyboard 24/7.

A NOTE FROM KELLY

Thank you very much for reading The Ghost of Branden Bay. Why not try the next book...

It's Branden Bay's Halloween Ball and Becky has been stood up by H who is tied up with a murder case in Devon. Arriving at Branden Bay Castle alone, Becky bumps into Connor Davies. But while standing on the steps of the castle he is shot and soon in a critical condition in hospital. The only witness to the murder is the castle's resident ghost. Can Becky connect to the spirit to find the truth before the killer comes for her too?

If you would like to join my mailing list and be alerted of my new releases and receive a free digital copy of my novella about Becky's grandma Constance, then please visit my website at www.kellymasonbooks.com

Reviews are really helpful to an author so please leave one on Amazon or Goodreads if you have a few moments.

Made in United States
Orlando, FL
21 September 2022

22659509R00159